COMEDIANS

JOHN L'HEUREUX

PENGUIN BOOKS

PENGUIN BOOKS
Published by the Penguin Group
Viking Penguin, a division of Penguin Books USA Inc.,
375 Hudson Street, New York, New York 10014, U.S.A.
Penguin Books Ltd, 27 Wrights Lane, London W8 5TZ, England
Penguin Books Australia Ltd, Ringwood, Victoria, Australia
Penguin Books Canada Ltd, 10 Alcorn Avenue, Suite 300,
Toronto, Ontario, Canada M4V 3B2
Penguin Books (N.Z.) Ltd, 182–190 Wairau Road,
Auckland 10, New Zealand

Penguin Books Ltd, Registered Offices:
Harmondsworth, Middlesex, England

First published in the United States of America by
Viking Penguin, a division of Penguin Books USA Inc., 1990
Published in Penguin Books 1992

10 9 8 7 6 5 4 3 2 1

PUBLISHER'S NOTE
These stories are works of fiction. Names, characters, places,
and incidents either are the product of the author's imagination or are used fictitiously, and any resemblance to actual persons, living or dead, events, or locales is entirely coincidental.

"The Comedian" first appeared in *The Atlantic Monthly;*
"Father" in *The Los Angeles Times Magazine;* "The Expert on
God" in *Epoch;* "Themselves" in *ZYZZYVA;* "Mutti" in *The
Village Voice;* and "Maria Luz Buenvida" in *The Critic.* "Sources"
was published under the auspices of the P.E.N. Syndicated
Fiction Project.

THE LIBRARY OF CONGRESS HAS CATALOGUED THE HARDCOVER AS FOLLOWS:
L'Heureux, John.
Comedians/John L'Heureux.
p. cm.
ISBN 0-670-82918-8 (hc.)
ISBN 0 14 01.6765 X (pbk.)
I. Title
PS3562.H4C66 1990
813'.54—dc20   89–40338

Printed in the United States of America
Set in Garamond Number 3
Designed by Fritz A. Metsch

For my wife,
Joan Polston L'Heureux

"Comedy is an escape not from truth but from despair."
—*Christopher Fry*

ACKNOWLEDGMENTS

Some of the stories in this collection appeared previously in *The Atlantic Monthly, The Boston Review, Critic, Epoch, Los Angeles Times Literary Supplement, Mānoa, Village Voice Literary Supplement,* and *Zyzzyva.*

"The Comedian" has been reprinted in *Prize Stories: The O. Henry Awards, 1986; The Substance of Things Hoped For* (Doubleday, 1987); and *The Contemporary Atlantic: Best of the Decade* (Atlantic Monthly Press, 1988).

CONTENTS

I: THE COMEDIAN

Corinne hasn't planned to have a baby. She is thirty-eight and happy and she wants to get on with it. She is a stand-up comedian with a husband, her second, and with no thought of a child, and what she wants out of life now is a lot of laughs. To give them, and especially to get them. And here she is, by accident, pregnant.

The doctor sees her chagrin and is surprised, because he thinks of her as a competent and sturdy woman. But that's how things are these days and so he suggests an abortion. Corinne says she'll let him know; she has to do some thinking. A baby.

"That's great," Russ says. "If you want it, I mean. I want it. I mean, I want it if you do. It's up to you, though. You know what I mean?"

And so they decide that, of course, they will have the baby, of course they want the baby, the baby is just exactly what they need.

In the bathroom mirror that night, Russ looks through his eyes into his cranium for a long time. Finally he sees his mind. As he watches, it knots like a fist. And he continues to watch, glad, as that fist beats the new baby flat and thin, a dead slick silverfish.

Mother. Mother and baby. A little baby. A big baby. Bouncing babies. At once Corinne sees twenty babies, twenty pink basketball babies, bouncing down the court and then up into the air and—whoosh—they swish neatly through the net. Babies.

Baby is its own excuse for being. Or is it? Well, Corinne was a Catholic right up until the end of her first marriage, so she thinks maybe it is. One thing is sure: the only subject you can't make a good joke about is abortion.

Yes, they will have the baby. Yes, she will be the mother. Yes.

But the next morning, while Russ is at work, Corinne turns off the television and sits on the edge of the couch. She squeezes her thighs together, tight; she contracts her stomach; she arches her back. This is no joke. This is the real thing. By an act of will, she is going to expel this baby, this invader, this insidious little murderer. She pushes and pushes and nothing happens. She pushes again, hard. And once more she pushes. Finally she gives up and lies back against the sofa, resting.

After a while she puts her hand on her belly, and as she does so, she is astonished to hear singing.

It is the baby. It has a soft reedy voice and it sings slightly off-key. Corinne listens to the words: "Some of these days, you'll miss me, honey. . . ."

Corinne faints then, and it is quite some time before she wakes up.

When she wakes, she opens her eyes only a slit and looks carefully from left to right. She sits on the couch, vigilant, listening, but she hears nothing. After a while she says three Hail Marys and an Act of Contrition, and then, confused and a little embarrassed, she does the laundry.

She does not tell Russ about this.

· · ·

Well, it's a time of strain, Corinne tells herself, even though in California there isn't supposed to be any strain. Just surfing and tans and divorce and a lot of interfacing. No strain and no babies.

Corinne thinks for a second about interfacing babies, but forces the thought from her mind and goes back to thinking about her act. Sometimes she does a very funny set on interfacing, but only if the audience is middle-aged. The younger ones don't seem to know that interfacing is laughable. Come to think of it, *nobody* laughs much in California. Everybody smiles, but who laughs?

Laughs: that's something she can use. She does Garbo's laugh: "I am so hap-py." What was that movie? "I am so happy." She does the Garbo laugh again. Not bad. Who else laughs? Joe E. Brown. The Wicked Witch of the West. Who was she? Somebody Hamilton. Will anybody remember these people? Ruth Buzzi? Goldie Hawn? Yes, that great giggle. Of course, the best giggle is Burt Reynolds's. High and fey. Why does he do that? Is he sending up his own image?

Corinne is thinking of images, Burt Reynolds's and Tom Selleck's, when she hears singing: "Cal-i-for-nia, here I come, Right back where I started from. . . ." Corinne stops pacing and stands in the doorway to the kitchen—as if I'm waiting for the earthquake, she thinks. But there is no earthquake; there is only the thin sweet voice, singing.

Corinne leans against the doorframe and listens. She closes her eyes. At once it is Easter, and she is a child again at Sacred Heart Grammar School, and the thirty-five members of the children's choir, earnest and angelic, look out at her from where they stand, massed about the altar. They wear red cassocks and white surplices, starched, and they seem to have descended from heaven for this one occasion. Their voices are pure, high, untouched by adolescence or by pain; and, with a conviction born of absolute innocence, they sing to God and to Corinne, "Cal-i-for-nia, here I come."

Corinne leans against the doorframe and listens truly now. Imagination aside, drama aside—she listens. It is a single voice she hears, thin and reedy. So, she did not imagine it the first time. It is true. The baby sings.

. . .

That night, when Russ comes home, he takes his shower, and they settle in with their first martini and everything is cozy.

Corinne asks him about his day, and he tells her. It was a lousy day. Russ started his own construction company a year ago just as the bottom fell out of the building business, and now there are no jobs to speak of. Just renovation stuff. Cleanup after fires. Sometimes Victorian restorations down in the gay district. But that's about it. So whatever comes his way is bound to be lousy. This is Russ's second marriage, though, so he knows not to go too far with a lousy day. Who needs it?

"But I've got you, babe," he says, and pulls her toward him, and kisses her.

"We've got each other," Corinne says, and kisses him back. "And the baby," she says.

He holds her close then, so that she can't see his face. She makes big eyes like an actor in a bad comedy—she doesn't know why; she just always sees the absurd in everything. After a while they pull away, smiling, secret, and sip their martinis.

"Do you know something?" she says. "Can I tell you something?"

"What?" he says. "Tell me."

"You won't laugh?"

"No," he says, laughing. "I'm sorry. No, I won't laugh."

"Okay," she says. "Here goes."

There is a long silence, and then he says, "Well?"

"It sings."

"It sings?"

"The baby. The fetus. It sings."

Russ is stalled, but only for a second. Then he says, "Rock and roll? Or plainchant?" He begins to laugh, and he laughs so hard that he chokes and sloshes martini onto the couch. "You're wonderful," he says. "You're really a funny, funny girl. Woman." He laughs some more. "Is that for your act? I love it."

"I'm serious," she says. "I mean it."

"Well, it's great," he says. "They'll love it."

Corinne puts her hand on her stomach and thinks she has never been so alone in her life. She looks at Russ, with his big square jaw and all those white teeth and his green eyes so trusting and innocent, and she realizes for one second how corrupt she is, how lost, how deserving of a baby who sings; and then she pulls herself together because real life has to go on.

"Let's eat out," she says. "Spaghetti. It's cheap." She kisses him gently on his left eyelid, on his right. She gazes into his eyes and smiles, so that he will not guess she is thinking: Who is this man? Who am I?

Corinne has a job, Fridays and Saturdays for the next three weeks, at the Ironworks. It's not The Comedy Shop, but it's a legitimate gig, and the money is good. Moreover, it will give her something to think about besides whether or not she should go through with the abortion. She and Russ have put that on hold.

She is well into her third month, but she isn't showing yet, so she figures she can handle the three weekends easily. She wishes, in a way, that she were showing. As it is, she only looks. . . . She searches for the word, but not for long. The word is *fat*. She looks fat.

She could do fat-girl jokes, but she hates jokes that put down women. And she hates jokes that are blue. Jokes that ridicule husbands. Jokes that ridicule the joker's looks. Jokes about nationalities. Jokes that play into audience prejudice. Jokes about the terrible small town you came from. Jokes about how poor you were, how ugly, how unpopular. Phyllis Diller jokes. Joan Rivers jokes. Jokes about small boobs, wrinkles, sexual inadequacy. Why is she in this business? she wonders. She hates jokes.

She thinks she hears herself praying: Please, please.

What should she do at the Ironworks? What should she do about the baby? What should she do?

The baby is the only one who's decided what to do. The baby sings.

Its voice is filling out nicely and it has enlarged its repertoire considerably. It sings a lot of classical melodies Corinne thinks she remembers from somewhere, churchy stuff, but it also favors golden oldies from the forties and fifties, with a few real old-timers thrown in when they seem appropriate. Once, right at the beginning, for instance, after Corinne and Russ had quarreled, Corinne locked herself in the bathroom to sulk and after a while was surprised, and then grateful, to hear the baby crooning, "Oh, my man, I love him so." It struck Corinne a day or so later that this could be a baby that would sell out for *any* one-liner . . . if indeed she decided to have the baby . . . and so she was relieved when the baby turned to more classical pieces.

The baby sings only now and then, and it sings better at some times than at others, but Corinne is convinced it sings best on weekend evenings when she is preparing for her gig. Before she leaves home, Corinne always has a long hot soak in the tub. She lies in the suds with her little orange bath pillow at her head and, as she runs through the night's possibilities, preparing ad-libs, heckler put-downs, segues, the baby sings to her.

There is some connection, she is sure, between her work and the baby's singing, but she can't guess what it is. It doesn't matter. She loves this: just she and the baby, together, in song.

Thank you, thank you, she prays.

. . . .

The Ironworks gig goes extremely well. It is a young crowd, mostly, and so Corinne sticks to her young jokes: life in California, diets, dating, school. The audience laughs, and Russ says she is better than ever, but at the end of the three weeks the manager tells her, "You got it, honey. You got all the moves. You really make them laugh, you know? But they laugh from here only"—he taps his head—"not from the gut. You gotta get gut. You know? Like feeling."

So now the gig is over and Corinne lies in her tub trying to think of gut. She's gotta get gut, she's gotta get feeling. Has she ever *felt*? Well, she feels for Russ; she loves him. She felt for Alan, that bastard; well, maybe he wasn't so bad; maybe he just wasn't ready for marriage, any more than she was. Maybe it's California; maybe nobody *can* feel in California.

Enough about feeling, already. Deliberately, she puts feeling out of her mind, and calls up babies instead. A happy baby, she thinks, and at once the bathroom is crowded with laughing babies, each one roaring and carrying on like Ed McMahon. A fat baby, and she sees a Shelley Winters baby, an Elizabeth Taylor baby, an Orson Welles baby. An active baby: a mile of trampolines and babies doing quadruple somersaults, back flips, high dives. A healthy baby: babies lifting weights, swimming the Channel. Babies.

But abortion is the issue, not babies. Should she have it, or not?

At once she sees a bloody mess, a crushed-looking thing, half animal, half human. Its hands open and close. She gasps. "No," she says aloud, and shakes her head to get rid of the awful picture. "No," and covers her face.

Gradually she realizes that she has been listening to humming, and now the humming turns to song—"It ain't necessarily so," sung in a good clear mezzo.

Her eyes hurt and she has a headache. In fact, her eyes hurt all the time.

.   .   .

Corinne has finally convinced Russ that she hears the baby singing. Actually, he is convinced that Corinne is halfway around the bend with worry, and he is surprised, when he thinks about it, to find that he loves her anyway, crazy or not. He tells her that as much as he hates the idea, maybe she ought to think about having an abortion.

"I've actually gotten to like the singing," she says.

"Corinne," he says.

"It's the things I see that scare me to death."

"What things? What do you see?"

At once she sees a little crimson baby. It has been squashed into a mason jar. The tiny eyes almost disappear into the puffed cheeks, the cheeks into the neck, the neck into the torso. It is a pickled baby, ancient, preserved.

"Tell me," he says.

"Nothing," she says. "It's just that my eyes hurt."

.   .   .

It's getting late for an abortion, the doctor says, but she can still have one safely.

He's known her for twenty years, all through the first marriage and now through this one, and he's puzzled that a funny and sensible girl like Corinne should be having such a tough time with pregnancy. He had recommended abortion right from the start, because she didn't seem to want the baby and because she was almost forty, but he hadn't really expected her to take him up on it. Looking at her now, though, it is clear to him that she'll never make it. She'll be wacko—if not during the pregnancy, then sure as hell afterward.

So what does she think? What does Russ think?

Well, first, she explains in her new, sort of wandering way, there's something else she wants to ask about; not really important, she supposes, but just something, well, kind of different she probably should mention. It's the old problem of the baby . . . well, um, singing.

"Singing?" he asks.

"Singing?" he asks again.

"And humming," Corinne says.

They sit in silence for a minute, the doctor trying to decide whether or not this is a joke. She's got this great poker face. She really is a good comic. So after a while he laughs, and then when she laughs, he knows he's done the right thing. But what a crazy sense of humor!

"You're terrific," he says. "Anything else? How's Russ? How was the Ironworks job?"

"My eyes hurt," she says. "I have headaches."

And so they discuss her vision for a while, and stand-up comedy, and she makes him laugh. And that's that.

At the door he says to her, "Have an abortion, Corinne. Now, before it's too late."

.　.　.

They have just made love and now Russ puts off the light and they lie together in the dark, his hand on her belly.

"Listen," he says. "I want to say something. I've been thinking about what the doctor said, about an abortion. I hate it, I hate the whole idea, but you know, we've got to think of you. And I think this baby is too much for you, I think maybe that's why you've been having those headaches and stuff. Don't you think?"

Corinne puts her hand on his hand and says nothing. After a long while Russ speaks again, into the darkness.

"I've been a lousy father. Two sons I never see. I never see them. The stepfather's good to them, though; he's a good father. I thought maybe I'd have another chance at it, do it right this time, like the marriage. Besides, the business isn't always going to be this bad, you know; I'll get jobs; I'll get money. We could afford it, you know? A son. A daughter. It would be nice. But what I mean is, we've got to take other things into consideration, we've got to consider your health. You're not strong enough, I guess. I always think of you as strong, because you do those gigs and you're funny and all, but, I mean, you're almost forty, and the doctor thinks that maybe an abortion is the way to go, and what do I know. I don't know. The singing. The headaches. I don't know."

Russ looks into the dark, seeing nothing.

"I worry about you, you want to know the truth? I do. Corinne?"

Corinne lies beside him, listening to him, refusing to listen to the baby, who all this time has been singing. Russ is as alone as she is, even more alone. She is dumbfounded. She is speechless with love. If he were a whirlpool, she thinks, she would fling herself into it. If he were . . . but he is who he is, and she loves only him, and she makes her decision.

"You think I'm losing my mind," she says.

Silence.

"Yes."

More silence.

"Well, I'm not. Headaches are a normal part of lots of pregnancies, the doctor told me, and the singing doesn't mean anything at all. He explained what was really going on, why I thought I heard it sing. You see," Corinne says, improvising freely now, making it all up, for him, her gift to him, "you see, when you get somebody as high-strung as me and you add pregnancy right at the time I'm about to make it big as a stand-up, then the pressures get to be so much that sometimes the imagination can take over, the doctor said, and when you tune in to the normal sounds of your body, you hear them really loud, as if they were amplified by a three-thousand-watt PA system, and it can sound like singing. See?"

Russ says nothing.

"So you see, it all makes sense, really. You don't have to worry about me."

"Come on," Russ says. "Do you mean to tell me you never heard the baby singing?"

"Well, I heard it, sort of. You know? It was really all in my mind. I mean, the *sound* was in my body physiologically, but my hearing it as *singing* was just . . ."

"Just your imagination."

Corinne does not answer.

"Well?"

"Right," she says, making the total gift. "It was just my imagination."

And the baby—who has not stopped singing all this time, love songs mostly—stops singing now, and does not sing again until the day scheduled for the abortion.

. . .

The baby has not sung in three weeks. It is Corinne's fifth month now, and at last they have been able to do an amniocentesis. The news is bad. One of the baby's chromosomes does not match up to anything in hers, anything in Russ's. What this means, they tell her, is that the baby is not normal. It will be deformed in some way; in what way, they have no idea.

Corinne and Russ decide on abortion.

They talk very little about their decision now that they have made it. In fact, they talk very little about anything. Corinne's face grows daily more haggard, and Corinne avoids Russ's eyes. She is silent much of the time, thinking. The baby is silent all the time.

The abortion will be by hypertonic saline injection, a simple procedure, complicated only by the fact that Corinne has waited so long. She has been given a booklet to read and she has listened to a tape, and so she knows about the injection of the saline solution, she knows about the contractions that will begin slowly and then get more and more frequent, and she knows about the dangers of infection and excessive bleeding.

She knows moreover that it will be a formed fetus she will expel.

Russ has come with her to the hospital and is outside in the waiting room. Corinne thinks of him, of how she loves him, of how their lives will be better, safer, without this baby who sings. This deformed baby. Who sings. If only she could hear the singing once more, just once.

Corinne lies on the table with her legs in the thigh rests, and one of the nurses drapes the examining sheet over and around her. The other nurse, or someone—Corinne is getting confused; her eyesight seems fuzzy—takes her pulse and her blood pressure. She feels someone washing her, the careful hands, the warm fluid. So, it is beginning.

Corinne closes her eyes and tries to make her mind a blank. Dark, she thinks. Dark. She squeezes her eyes tight against the light, she wants to remain in this cool darkness forever, she wants to cease being. And then, amazingly, the dark does close in on her. Though she opens her eyes, she sees nothing. She can remain this way forever if she wills it. The dark is cool to the touch, and it is comforting somehow; it invites her in. She can lean into it, give herself up to it, and be safe, alone, forever.

She tries to sit up. She will enter this dark. She will do it. Please, please, she hears herself say. And then all at once she thinks of Russ and the baby, and instead of surrendering to the dark, she pushes it away.

With one sweep of her hand she pushes the sheet from her and flings it to the floor. She pulls her legs from the thigh rests and manages to sit up, blinded still, but fighting.

"Here now," a nurse says, caught off guard, unsure what to do. "Hold on now. It's all right. It's fine."

"Easy now. Easy," the doctor says, thinking Yes, here it is, what else is new.

Together the nurses and the doctor make an effort to stop her, but they are too late, because by this time Corinne has fought free of any restraints. She is off the examining couch and, naked, huddles in the corner of the small room.

"No," she shouts. "I want the baby. I want the baby." And later, when she has stopped shouting, when she has stopped crying, still she clutches her knees to her chest and whispers over and over, "I want the baby."

So there is no abortion after all.

By the time she is discharged, Corinne's vision has re-

turned, dimly. Moreover, though she tells nobody, she has
heard humming, and once or twice a whole line of music.
The baby has begun to sing again.

. . .

Corinne has more offers than she wants: The Hungry I, The
Purple Onion, The Comedy Shop. Suddenly everybody de-
cides it's time to take a look at her, but she is in no shape to
be looked at, so she signs for two weeks at My Uncle's Bureau
and lets it go at that.

She is only marginally pretty now, she is six months pregnant, and she is carrying a deformed child. Furthermore, she can
see very little, and what she does see, she often sees double.

Her humor, therefore, is spare and grim, but audiences
love it. She begins slow: "When I was a girl, I always wanted
to look like Elizabeth Taylor," she says, and glances down at
her swollen belly. Two beats. "And now I do." They laugh
with her, and applaud. Now she can quicken the pace,
sharpen the humor. They follow her; they are completely
captivated.

She has found some new way of holding her body—tipping
her head, thrusting out her belly—and instead of putting off
her audience, or embarrassing them, it charms them. The
laughter is *with* her, the applause *for* her. She could do anything out there and get away with it. And she knows it. They
simply love her.

In her dressing room after the show she tells herself that
somehow, magically, she's learned to work from the heart
instead of just from the head. She's got gut. She's got feeling.
But she knows it's something more than that.

By the end of the two weeks she is convinced that the
successful new element in her act is the baby. This deformed
baby, the abnormal baby she has tried to get rid of. And what
interests her most is that she no longer cares about success
as a stand-up.

16

Corinne falls asleep that night to the sound of the baby's crooning. She is trying to pray, Please, please, but with Russ's snoring and the baby's lullaby, they all get mixed up together in her mind—God, Russ, the baby—and she forgets to whom she is praying or why. She sleeps.

.   .   .

The baby sings all the time now. It starts first thing in the morning with a nice soft piece by Telemann or Brahms; there are assorted lullabies at bedtime; and throughout the day it is bop, opera, ragtime, blues, a little rock and roll, big-band stuff—the baby never tires.

Corinne tells no one about this, not even Russ.

She and Russ talk about almost everything now: their love for each other, their hopes for the baby, their plans. They have lots of plans. Russ has assured Corinne that whatever happens, he's ready for it. Corinne is his whole life, and no matter how badly the baby is deformed, they'll manage. They'll do the right thing. They'll survive.

They talk about almost everything, but they do not talk about the baby's singing.

For Corinne the singing is secret, mysterious. It contains some revelation, of course, but she does not want to know what that revelation might be.

The singing is somehow tied up with her work; but more than that, with her life. It is part of her fate. It is inescapable. And she is perfectly content to wait.

.   .   .

Corinne has been in labor for three hours, and the baby has been singing the whole time. The doctor has administered a mild anesthetic and a nurse remains at bedside, but the birth does not seem imminent, and so for Corinne it is a period of pain and waiting. And for the baby, singing.

"These lights are so strong," Corinne says, or thinks she says. "The lights are blinding."

The nurse looks at her for a moment and then goes back to the letter she is writing.

"Please," Corinne says, "thank you."

She is unconscious, she supposes; she is imagining the lights. Or perhaps the lights are indeed bright and she sees them as they really are *because* she is unconscious. Or perhaps her sight has come back, as strong as it used to be. Whatever the case, she doesn't want to think about it right now. Besides, for some reason or other, even though the lights are blinding, they are not blinding her. They do not even bother her. It is as if light is her natural element.

"Thank you," she says. To someone.

The singing is wonderful, a cappella things Corinne recognizes as Brahms, Mozart, Bach. The baby's voice can assume any dimension it wants now, swelling from a single thin note to choir volume; it can take on the tone and resonance of musical instruments, violin, viola, flute; it can become all sounds; it enchants.

The contractions are more frequent; even unconscious, Corinne can tell that. Good. Soon the waiting will be over and she will have her wonderful baby, her perfect baby. But at once she realizes hers will not be a perfect baby; it will be deformed. "Please," she says, "please," as if prayer can keep Russ from being told—as he will be soon after the birth— that his baby has been born dumb. Russ, who has never understood comedians.

But now the singing has begun to swell in volume. It is as if the baby has become a full choir, with many voices, with great strength.

The baby will be fine, however it is, she thinks. She thinks of Russ, worried half to death. She is no longer worried. She accepts what will be.

The contractions are very frequent now and the light is much brighter. She knows the doctor has come into the room, because she hears his voice. There is another nurse too. And soon there will be the baby.

The light is so bright that she can see none of them. She can see into the light, it is true; she can see the soft fleecy nimbus glowing beyond the light, but she can see nothing in the room.

The singing. The singing and the light. It is Palestrina she hears, in polyphony, each voice lambent. The light envelops her, catches her up from this table where the doctor bends over her and where already can be seen the shimmering yellow hair of the baby. The light lifts her, and the singing lifts her, and she says, "Yes," she says, "Thank you."

She accepts what will be. She accepts what is.

The room is filled with singing and with light, and the singing is transformed into light, more light, more lucency, and still she says, "Yes," until she cannot bear it, and she reaches up and tears the light aside. And sees.

II: BRIEF LIVES

FATHER

Long before he got sick, our father was down there in the cellar painting away. He had rigged up an easel for himself and suspended a couple naked light bulbs from a beam—to simulate northern light, he said—and he painted things from photographs and magazines and books. Later he painted things vaguely reminiscent of what he had seen on walks. At the beginning of the end he painted things nobody except himself had ever seen before. He claimed that his painting style simply evolved from representational to impressionistic to a kind of hard-edged expressionism of his own. But long before we understood what he was doing, our father had begun to escape from us. He was in the process of disappearing.

John, who is artistic, was the first to notice the hairline crack in each of the paintings. Our father was all done with his representational period. He had lined up a whole bunch of the things in the cellar, propped against the washer and dryer and the boiler and the old bikes. They were everywhere, stacked two and three deep, because he was having a sort of show, a retrospective as it were, for John and Joan who were visiting home from California where he teaches writing and she teaches English. John and Joan have no children. They don't go in for that sort of thing. Or perhaps they can't. In any case they were admiring the pictures generally, sometimes pointing out a special thing about one or another, and our father was standing by, very serious, as they assessed what they liked or disliked about his creations. All of a sudden John said, "Look at this. *Look* at this." He ran a long skinny finger down an invisible crack in a picture. And then in another. And in another.

At the time our father just stood there, not doddering yet, not even a little bit dingy, just smiling as if he were getting some secret pleasure out of John's discovery. There's no telling just how much he was planning or how much he was deceiving us at that point; he was still in his impressionistic period. But there was no question that John was right: there was this line, wiggly sometimes and at other times jagged like a bolt of lightning and at all times almost invisible. It ran down the center of the painting as if it were a warning or a threat or a prophecy.

"A theme," John said. "A recurrent theme, as if your impression of the world reflected the primal fall or as if you saw that it might all come apart at any minute."

We laughed at that because it sounded so important, and

our father laughed, and then we all went upstairs for a drink and dinner.

Not long after this he moved into his expressionist period, where people seemed less than whole and things no longer looked like what they were. He used a lot of dark colors in this period, though some had a grim brilliance that made us look at them, and look again. Huge rocks began to appear in his paintings, boulders practically, hovering in the air as if they might fall out of the picture any minute and crush us. And those cracks down the center began to get bigger. We could see them clearly now, even from a few feet off. Everything was distorted. What he was expressing wasn't very nice, even in the abstract.

Later when our father was diagnosed as Parkinson's, and well advanced too, he went on heavy doses of L-dopa that controlled the shaking and allowed him to continue to paint. That seemed fine, because it kept him occupied and out of our mother's way. He was deteriorating fast. And he was driving her crazy with things like putting the kettle on while she was out for groceries and forgetting it until it melted down flat to the burner. "He could have burned the house down," she would scream, while he flinched at the sound, "he could have burned himself to death," and then she would cry and scream and cry some more, until she had enough strength to go on. We were less patient with her than we should have been because we just didn't know how bad off our father was or what it was like for her to never have a quiet thought, midnight or morning, for years as she took care of him. When she finished her scene, our father would dodder on down the stairs and paint away. It was very near the end.

He had been in his expressionist period for quite a while when John and Joan came to visit again. They stayed in the house for a week with our father and mother and got a close look at the way things were. At first John was horrified at what had happened to our father physically: the stumble when he tried to walk, the wandering mind, the uncompleted sentence. And at our mother who seemed half-lunatic.

On the first morning, for instance, at breakfast time, she was shuffling in her bunny slippers from the stove to the table and all of a sudden she stopped dead. She let out a long scream and pulled her hair back from her temples, wailing, "Oh God, oh God, *now* you see what I have to put up with." John pushed away from the table and ran to her and said, "What? What is it?" And she cried out, in tears, in despair, "I already *stirred* his orange juice. I try to save him. I try. I try." John looked over at our father, who was clinking the glass as he tried to stir the orange juice with a fork, and he looked down at our mother, who was sobbing helplessly against his chest, and he looked over at Joan, who was looking the way Joan does, which we have frankly never figured out, and he said, "Something has to be done here. But what? What?"

After breakfast John took a look at the new paintings and, as he admitted later, he should have noticed how things were. Each picture had a thousand different fractures but there was something new; in the center, a kind of dark cave opened up into the canvas. "You could hide there," John said. "You could disappear forever." The newest painting stood unfinished on the easel, the same dark colors with their odd brilliance, the same fractures, fissures, cracks, but in the middle where that dark cave should be, there was empty canvas. Our father had left an absence in the center of things, for later.

The days that week were very long, John said. Our mother slept sometimes but mostly she raved like a madwoman, in desperation and devotion to our father, who merely sat, silent, or went for slow slow painful walks with John. The days were all right and the evenings were all right but at night our father was impossible. Sitting with them in the living room, like old times, he would nod and smile and make a little rambling comment now and then, but when they wanted to help him to bed, they found he had become nearly paralyzed. His limbs would not bend, they were like stone, and John and Joan together could barely move him. But they had method. They would pry him from his chair, pulling and pushing until they got him upright, and then they staggered him between them to his bed. He was bones only, but he was heavy beyond belief. Our mother would scuffle around saying, "See? Do you see?" and run ahead to ready the pillows, to pull down the sheet and blankets the way he liked, then "Do you see?" It took an hour to get him into bed.

"This is not the worst of it," our mother said. "You don't know. He pees in the wastebasket. He does. In the night he gets afraid of the toilet. So help me God." John laughed and our mother laughed and said, "I'm not crazy yet, I guess, because I still know it's funny . . . in a way. And once he's up, you never know what he'll do. He'll boil water and burn us down or go out on the street in the middle of the night— he's done it more than once—and there's no one who cares or who can help. . . ."

She stopped then because our father suddenly appeared from bed, stood smiling at the door, and moved across the room to his favorite chair, walking easily now, his limbs unstuck. "Oh no," she said, "don't let him sit. He'll fall asleep and we'll never get him up." And she was right. In less than a minute he slumped down into sleep and they had to go through it all again: prying him from the chair, getting him upright, staggering him down the hall to his bed. It was exhausting. It was frightening.

"How is this possible?" John said. "He was stiff as a board and out like a light, and it took an hour to get him into bed, and then minutes later he appears as if he's all set for a jaunt in the country. This isn't possible."

Our mother laughed this time, with bitterness and gratitude that someone saw at last what it was like, but before they could even get a drink and try to recover, there he was again. She ran ahead to do the pillows, but she was seventy-six and nearly done herself, and as they were staggering him to bed, she came apart, and shouted, "Bastard life, what kind of bastard life is this? I want out, I want out, I want out," but there was no way out, and she knew it, so she hurled herself into the hall closet, and tore the clothes from hangers and threw the hangers on the floor and, screaming, crouched there in a wretched corner, screaming still. Our father, paralyzed and dumb, snapped out of it and said to Joan, "That poor woman, that poor woman," and tears came as he said, "she'll die."

The next morning when our father went downstairs to paint, John made arrangements for a Home, and then he called us to our father's house and gave a speech. Our mother cowered in a chair.

"We must not deceive ourselves," he said. "We are sentencing our father to death. Because he is old and dotty and frail and cannot be responsible for wandering or peeing in the night, we say yes, this is impossible, he must have specialized care. But what we are *really* saying is: we cannot cope with this, so we must put him away. And he defies us, our pretensions and excuses and our lies." John teaches writing. He stands like a professor, wringing his hands as if that way he could squeeze the instincts out of them. "He defies us," John said, "by being, now and then, shockingly rational and sane and simple. One minute, we think he's lost it. The next, with his words and with his smile and with his knowing acceptance of this impossible situation, he tells us that we are putting out of our sight and our concern a living, feeling, suffering human person—who is *my* father and *your* father and *your* husband—and on and on until we can never forget and, if we are honest, never forgive ourselves. Something must be done here. But what? What?"

Thus, it was settled. Our father would be put in a Home and our mother would be saved, in a sense, and we would all live with what had to be done.

John went downstairs to get him, to tell him how it was, to break the hard news. And then we all went down. But our father was not there.

The paintings were there, spread around the cellar, the huge boulders in them ready to fall on us, the fractured surfaces, the dark caves. But our father was not there. He was gone.

His last canvas stood on the easel, finished now but unlike any of the others. In the center where there should have been a cave, there was the door our father had gone through. The door stood open to a silver night. He had disappeared. He had escaped, leaving us with all our business incomplete, our goodness, understanding.

In the end our father painted clear untroubled air and, quicker than our love, he entered it.

THE EXPERT ON GOD

From the start faith had been a problem for him, and his recent ordination had changed almost nothing. His doubts were simply more appropriate to the priesthood now. That was the only difference.

As a child of ten he was saying his evening prayers when it suddenly struck him that Catholics believed in three gods, God the Father, God the Son, and God the Holy Ghost. He blushed and covered his face. What if the kids at school found out? They were Protestants, and therefore wrong, but at least they had only one God. Instantly it came to him that there were three *Persons* in one God. It was a mystery. He was very embarrassed but very relieved, and he actually looked around to see if anyone had heard his thoughts, and for the rest of his life it remained for him a moment of great shame. At eighteen, when he entered the Jesuits, he got up his courage and told this story to his confessor, who laughed. Matters of faith, he decided then, were better kept secret.

There were other doubts. He doubted Christ's presence in the Eucharist. He prayed for faith, and some kind of faith came to him, because he left off doubting about the Eucharist and moved on to doubt other matters: the virginity of Mary, the divinity of Christ, and then later the humanity of Christ. At one time or another, he doubted every article of belief, but only for a while, and only one at a time. Faith demanded a different response to each mystery, he discovered, but doubt was always the same. The initial onslaught of doubt lasted for only a moment, a quick and breathtaking conviction that none of it was true, and then that conviction itself surrendered to doubt, leaving an awful lingering unspeakable ache.

In the end he doubted the love of God, and that doubt did not pass.

He was a popular priest but he had no friends. He kept other Jesuits at a distance, he forced them away. He had no time for the intimacies of his own kind, caught up as he was in his assault on God. He prayed for faith. And when that did not come, he prayed for hope. And when that did not come, he went on anyway, teaching, preaching, saying Mass at the odd parish whenever he was asked. That is how things stood with him on the day of the accident.

It was Christmas Day, not because Christmas is symbolic, but because that is when it happened. Snow had fallen for nearly a week, and then on Christmas Eve there had been hail and then rain and then a sudden freeze. The streets were ready.

He had said Mass at Our Lady of Victories and was driving back to the Jesuit house. It was almost noon and the sun was high. "It doesn't matter," he said. The air was clear and the day was bright after all that snow, and as he drove through the vast open countryside, he marveled again at the absence of God. "It doesn't matter anymore."

He had very nearly achieved a kind of trance, staring at the sun on the ice, trying to obliterate all thought. Suddenly, off to the side of the road, he saw a dark blue car turned half on its side and three boys huddled near it, looking at him as if he might be bringing help. He braked quickly, skidded in a half turn, and came to a stop. It was then that he noticed the tiny red sports car in the field on the opposite side of the road. It was crumpled nearly in two. The priest looked at the boys, but they only looked back, stunned. Finally one of them pointed to the red sports car.

He scrabbled through the glove compartment until he found the little vial of holy oils. He sprinted toward the car, following the wild track it had made as it spun through the snow, and when he got to it, he was not surprised to see the front end was completely demolished. He stooped and looked through the shattered window. The driver had been thrown to the side; the dashboard, crumpled back into the car, had pinned him, head down, in the passenger seat. The door hung on a single hinge, open a few inches but not wide enough for the priest to get in. The door would not give and he could not force it to open wider. He looked around a moment for help and saw that of course there was none; the boys huddling together across the street were too stupefied to help—or maybe they were injured, for all he knew.

He put the vial of oils in his pocket and jogged rapidly around the car. There was no way in. Somebody was inside, dying perhaps, and though he was only a few inches away, he could not reach him. It was maddening. He struck the car with his fist and sobbed suddenly in anger and frustration. Desperate then, he braced his back against the side of the car, pushing outward on the broken door and twisting, half crazy, until the hinge gave way. He squeezed himself into the car behind the driver's seat. He could hear a kind of gurgling sound from the man trapped beneath the dashboard. He edged across until he was behind the passenger seat and, with what strength he could muster, he pulled back on it until it snapped and broke loose. He climbed onto it so that he was behind the body. He squatted, doubled up, hunched over, scarcely able to breathe, but at last he got his arms around the body and eased it free of the dashboard.

It was a boy, in his new car, and he was still alive, or nearly. He made a sound that might have been a sigh or a groan. Blood trickled from his mouth. Still he did not die.

The priest held him in his arms. Crushed himself, he nonetheless managed to get the oils from his pocket and to wet his thumb with them and to place his thumb on the boy's bloody forehead, saying "I absolve you from all your sins. In the name of the Father and of the Son and of the Holy Ghost. Amen." Then he was silent.

There was no sound from outside the car, no ambulance wail, no curious viewers. They were in the middle of nowhere, he and this dying boy he held in his arms. He had touched the boy with the holy oils and he had offered him absolution for his sins, and something should have happened by now. Someone should have come to help. The boy should have died. Something. But there was silence only, and the boy's harsh, half-choked breathing.

He began to pray, aloud, which struck him as foolish: to be holding a dying boy in his arms and reciting rote prayers about our father in heaven, about holy Mary, mother of God. What could he do? What could he say at such a moment? What would God do at such a moment, if there were a God?

"Well, do it," he said aloud, and heard the fury in his voice. "Say something." But there was silence from heaven.

His doubts became certainty and he said, "It doesn't matter," but it did matter and he knew it. What could anyone say to this crushed, dying thing, he wondered. What would God say if he cared as much as I?

He shook with an involuntary sob then, and as he did, the boy shuddered in agony and choked on the blood that had begun to pour from his mouth. The priest could see death beginning to ease across the boy's face. And still he could say nothing.

The boy turned—some dying reflex—and his head tilted in the priest's arms, trusting, like a lover. And at once the priest, faithless, unrepentant, gave up his prayers and bent to him and whispered, fierce and burning, "I love you," and continued till there was no breath, "I love you, I love you, I love you."

THE POISON GIRLS

Scarpetti knew all along that they hated him. Three young women: intelligent, attractive, accomplished, and quite clearly gunning for him. But that was just how things were in this business. Every so often you had to deal with a force of nature or a message from hell. You learned to live with it.

Scarpetti's business was teaching people to write fiction. Or rather, since you can't teach people to have talent, his business was to show them where their work went wrong, and to help them get in touch with their strongest material, and now and then to praise stuff that turned out well. "Writing is a dirty business," he liked to say, "and nobody really has to do it. So if you can't take criticism of your work, get out now."

But these three were not about to take criticism and they certainly were not getting out. To the contrary, by the end of the first week they had formed a kind of power block: Coral, Pauline, and Ronette.

In the very first class Scarpetti had tangled with Coral. Her story was potentially good, he said, but she had a little problem with dialogue. She said nothing. He illustrated what he meant by reading some of the dialogue aloud. Then, without a trace of sarcasm, he explained that fiction was not sociology, that when characters talk, they shouldn't sound like they're reading a sociology textbook, that this held true especially for the realist fiction she was writing. Still she said nothing. Finally he told her straight out that the dialogue was ludicrous. "But, you see," Coral said, triumphant, "that's exactly the effect I was trying to achieve." Scarpetti threw up his hands.

He spent forever on a story by Pauline, trying to show her that it lacked basic clarity. She merely shook her head, no. Scarpetti's mouth went tight for a second and he said, patiently, "But you must have noticed that none of us in this room can agree on the actual events of the story, Pauline. Now, there must be some reason why all of us are confused. Do you see?" He said this at the start of the class, and again in the middle, and again, a little annoyed, near the end. Just before the final bell, Pauline spoke. "I think the story is perfectly clear," she said. At which Scarpetti suddenly found himself shouting, "We can't even figure out the fucking *facts,* Pauline." And while he pulled his hair and tried to think of some new way to get this across to her, she spoke once more. "Sixteen years," Pauline said. "I have been writing for sixteen years, and nobody has ever talked this way about my work."

Scarpetti threw up his hands and Pauline burst into tears. She never spoke to him again.

Ronette never spoke to him in the first place, though she spoke to the class, at least long enough to tell them she was writing from the vantage point of feminist mythology, which most of them would not understand. "This is not hostility to males," she said, "this is simply fact." Scarpetti told her that he had a little familiarity with many mythologies—or at least with Greek, Latin, Christian, and Old Norse—and he could probably understand feminist mythology if she cared to explain, but Ronette said, addressing the class, that it was not the kind of thing you could explain; it was the kind of thing you had to know. Women knew; men didn't. "I'm sorry about how that must sound," she said to the class, not sounding sorry at all, "but that's just how it is. Period." She threw up her hands, an imitation of Scarpetti, and she sat back in her chair, cool and completely satisfied. Coral and Pauline looked surprised for a minute at how easily Scarpetti could be handled. They had found a leader.

Scarpetti just smiled, not willing to tangle with this stuff, hell hath no fury, et cetera. That was when, for his private amusement, he named them the Poison Girls. They were sad, angry, and malicious, he told himself, and calling them the Poison Girls allowed him to live with being hated, at least in the abstract.

Scarpetti, as Director of the Writers Workshop, told himself many things that allowed him to continue in such high-risk work. He told himself that the really good writers always liked him, or at least respected what he did for them. He told himself that all of these writers were given large sums of money to come here and study, and he was just doing what he was paid for. He told himself that the good he consciously performed outweighed the injuries he inflicted by accident. And he had certain minimal virtues, he told himself. He was quick to apologize, eager to see the other viewpoint, ready always to admit he was mistaken. He told himself these things and he believed them. These things were true.

Meanwhile the Poison Girls continued on, silent, furious, glowing in their dark.

They gave up writing fiction and wrote other things instead. They wrote on the stalls in the women's room, they wrote anonymous letters to the Chairman and the Dean, they wrote hate notes to Scarpetti himself, brief and unsigned, threatening his life. They wanted him dead. They wanted to pay him back, to make him stop, to get rid of him for good.

What do they want, he said to himself, shrugging, as he tossed the hate notes into the trash. Still, that was how things were in this business. If you were going to teach writing, you had to expect now and then to deal with little problems. The Poison Girls were just part of the deal, he told himself, and he went on teaching, and trying to teach.

The year was nearly over when, for the first time in his life, Scarpetti saw that he was not dealing with hatred in the abstract. There would not be a second time. A second time was not required.

It was the last of the Dougal Lecture Series and Scarpetti strode onstage to introduce Iris Murdoch. He was wearing his new blue suit and his Perry Ellis shirt and his Somebody's tie, and he looked terrific, given his limitations. Moreover he felt terrific. It was the end of the year, nearly. It was his final intro. And it was Big Iris he was introducing, the smartest, most inventive, most truly wicked and exciting writer alive. It was an honor to introduce her; it was an honor to direct this writing program; hell, it was an honor to be alive.

He stepped up to the microphone and smiled a welcome— even his teeth felt terrific—while the audience quieted down and gave him their attention, smiling back. "I'm excited," he said, conversationally almost, and they laughed at that, "I'm excited to introduce to you tonight the smartest, most inventive, most truly wicked . . ." and he went on as if he were making it up on the spot and not just quoting himself, and as he spoke, he could see they loved the spontaneity of it, the honesty, the boyish enthusiasm of a good writer for a great one. He talked about Murdoch's virtues as a novelist, her variety, her imaginative thrust, her incandescent intelligence, her daunting productivity, and then he embarked on the most dangerous part of the intro: the long list of her books. He used no notes, of course. He was working from memory, a nicely subtle testimony to his familiarity with her work and his admiration for it. *"Under the Net,"* he said, *"The Flight from the Enchanter, The Bell, The Italian Girl, The Time of the Angels, An Accidental . . ."* but he hesitated and lost the title, because at that moment he saw the Poison Girls looking up at him with unmixed hatred in their eyes. The hatred was the same as it always was, no less venomous, no more, but from this little distance the three of them seemed to be offering him one single intensified look. For the first time, Scarpetti really saw them, and he saw too what they were looking at, and he knew that they saw him truly. Only a part of him, perhaps, but they saw that part exactly as it was.

For that long long moment they looked at him, and he looked at himself through their eyes, and that was the end of him.

He finished the introduction. Indeed, he made capital of his long hesitation—"even true love sometimes forgets," he said—and wound up the intro in high style. But it was the end for Scarpetti nonetheless.

There was a new Director. The Workshop flourished. Scarpetti continued to teach for a while, with enthusiasm that was clearly artificial and at times even desperate. He taught less well each year. His own writing stopped altogether. He became reclusive, antisocial, and he seemed to wither physically as well.

Scarpetti had always been a bit fanatic, they told themselves. Obsessive. A little mad. Eventually nobody bothered with him at all. He was so odd-looking and cynical, he had a rotten disposition. He was hateful, truly.

SOURCES

At the start of her career the choreographer had fashioned dances out of poems, a line of music, a book by Dr. Seuss; out of anything that touched her mind. No matter what her material, she was always an intellectual dancer. Later in her career she created dances that celebrated ancient mysteries: the riddle of Oedipus, the revenge of Clytemnestra, the orgiastic rites of Dionysus, the rape of Helen, the golden apples of the Hesperides, the ironic curse that fell upon Cassandra. Still later, she left pagan mythology and moved on to the fall of man, the Incarnation, the temptation in the desert, the gift of tongues: Christian mysteries.

She had not danced out the darker mysteries of her own psyche. But she was sixty-one now and ready to take possession of her deepest material. Her talent was ripe for it. Her stamina still held. The time had come to risk cutting closer to the bone. And yet she could not decide on the nature of this new dance: personal or public, a descent into the depths of her own soul or into the essence of the American experience.

At first she had intended to explore the truth behind all those lies she told her psychiatrist. But that would have meant looking straight into the mystery of her conventional upbringing: the drunken mother, the domineering father, the dreams of triumph and escape. She had spent her life trying to erase such memories. She could not, now, go back. Was this intellectual cowardice? A betrayal of her artistic integrity? In the end it seemed best to leave her own soul untroubled and to capture instead the soul of America. What that might be, or where, she had no idea, but she was determined to find out and make it dance.

Thus, on a warm October morning, wearing her pale yellow sack dress and her practical shoes, she set out to walk over Washington, alone and unencumbered, anonymous despite her fame. She walked randomly, guided only by instinct, and in this way discovered the Smithsonian, a major disappointment, and, after a long long walk, Ford's Theatre, a disappointment as well. A dance about Lincoln? About assassinations? Neither of these spoke of the soul of America, let alone plumbed its depth. Perhaps coming to Washington had been a mistake. Perhaps she should explore her own soul after all.

She would think about all this tomorrow. Right now the heat was overwhelming and she had walked far too much and she wanted a bath. She would call a cab. She stood in the filthy street outside Ford's Theatre and looked in both directions. There were no cabs, only miles of tour vans, those strange elongated cars that drove forever from site to site. As she hesitated, uncertain what to do, a man called out to her, "Hey, lady, want a mini-tour? Ten bucks," and stuck a thumb out at a dark green van, a twelve-seater. Chance, accident, serendipity. She decided to join the tour. "Just wait here," he said, and gave her a ticket marked Bus 24. "The tour's half done, but just show him this and you'll get the first half of the next tour." She had no idea what he was talking about, but it didn't matter. She had turned herself over to fate. This is how the best dances got discovered.

The choreographer stood in the shade of an electronics store and got her bearings. Ford's Theatre was across the street, to north and south was a slum of sorts, baking in this sun. The streets and sidewalks were filthy. A derelict lay in the next doorway, clutching a wine bottle half concealed in a torn paper bag. So this was historical Washington, the heartbeat of America. Dark green tour vans were parked along the curb. No drivers. No passengers. And yet little knots of tourists, with tickets in hand, stood sweating in the sun, waiting. Near her were a mother and son, conspicuously not talking, conspicuously above it all. This interested her and she gave them a sidelong glance.

The mother was in her late fifties, pale, wrinkled, with a kind of miserable and accusing look, as if the world had done her an injustice and she wanted it known.

The son was around thirty, thin and desperate-looking, with a pointy face and long brown hair curling over his collar. He wore a tan corduroy suit, a heavy embroidered vest, and a plaid shirt with a string tie. He must have been sweltering.

The choreographer looked away. He had chosen his clothes, she imagined, solely to infuriate his mother and had, without doubt, succeeded. She looked at him once more and saw that he was looking back at her. He had a furtive, anguished gaze, as if he were being pursued and knew he would be caught.

"A match?" he said to her, his voice raspy and barely audible. He held up a crushed cigarette and began to bend it back into shape. The choreographer shook her head, no, and the young man looked around, confused, at the small clusters of people waiting for the tourist van. His mother made a show of not looking at him. Ignoring her, he walked to the next doorway and stood over the derelict who lay there half-awake, clutching his paper bag, and asked him if he had a match. The derelict twitched a little and muttered something. The young man bent down close to him and shouted, furious, "A match, a match. I said, do you have a match?" The derelict nodded off.

Another van pulled up then. The driver got out and threw open the doors, an invitation, saying to nobody in particular, "Change of vehicles, please. Change of vehicles." The mother rushed to the open doors and then back to the driver and asked, "Is this the car for number twenty-four?" But he only smiled and said, "Change of vehicles," and she took her son's sleeve and rushed him with her to the van. She took the seat in the middle next to the window, and her son sat next to her, miserable. The others on the tour began to drift toward the van when yet another one pulled up. "Number twenty-four," the driver called to them, and they all climbed in. The choreographer got the seat farthest in the back, a position she liked.

They settled in quickly, and the driver had already started the van and was pulling out when someone said, "Those two people in that car ahead. They're supposed to be with us. They're number twenty-four too."

The driver stopped the van where it was, halfway out in the street, and ambled on up to the van ahead of him. There was a fuss. The woman wouldn't get out, she shook her head, she snapped her ticket at him. The driver just nodded and ambled off. He stood a few feet away, smiling placidly at the sky, accustomed to this kind of thing. Finally the woman scrambled out of the van, her face a violent red, but she refused to get into the van full of people until her son joined her. He was keeping an angry distance. They were both silent and furious and they played their parts as if they had been through this scene a hundred times. They stood staring at each other until, at some invisible signal, he came to her and she shoved him ahead into the van where he took a seat in the row just in front of the choreographer. The mother followed and, though she could have squeezed in next to the choreographer, she chose to sit in the aisle on the padded wheel-hump. This way she was seated beside her son.

The driver, who had finished looking at the sky, now came over to close the door and noticed where she was sitting. "You can't sit there, ma'am," he said. "There's a seat right behind you. You can't sit on the wheel-bump. It's illegal." He continued to lean in the window while she moved to the seat behind.

The choreographer had shifted over to make more room and now the mother took the seat directly behind her son. There was the scent of gardenias about her. She settled in for a moment and then, having made her decision, she shot her head forward and said, loudly, "It's too bad I can't sit on a wheel-bump next to my own son. It's too bad we had to lose the first car. We weren't in *this* car when we started the tour. We were in the other car." She looked hard at the driver who stood beside the van and listened, as he was meant to. "And then they left us waiting for one whole half hour at the Smithsonian, broiling in the sun. Every single person here can testify to that. We weren't with them. We were in the other car where we had good seats."

She drew a breath and hung there, leaning forward at her

son's ear, waiting for a response. But he made none at all.

The driver, seeing she was done, leaned in the window and said, "What?"

"Our seats," she said. "We had good seats in the first car, and we lost them, and then *that* man said to get in his car, and then you said to get out, and so twice now we've lost good seats."

"Oh," the driver said, softly. "Well, it won't be but five minutes that you'll be discomfited. You'll be out soon." He walked to the other side of the car and got in.

But she was not done. "It's too bad . . ."

"Stop doing that," her son said in a strangled voice. He did not look up. He did not turn around.

"Well, it's got to be said."

"I detest you."

"It's got to be said."

She sat back then and pushed against the choreographer, squirming a little to get good shoulder room. The scent of gardenias came from her again, sweet, with something acid underneath it that might have been gin, the choreographer thought, or simply malice.

"Arlington Cemetery next," the driver said, and as he drove off there was silence in the van.

Twice the woman leaned forward to say something, but thought better of it. The silence continued for three minutes, and then four, while everybody waited. The son did not move. Then she began to talk to him in a whisper, very rapidly, getting louder as she went on, her voice rising in volume with her indignation. Soon they all could hear her. ". . . and instead of doing his job, he went off to have coffee and I had to sling my own damn bag up on the luggage rack."

Sling, the choreographer said to herself. It didn't fit.

"And *he* was black *too*."

"Stop talking to me," the son said loudly, his head still bowed. "I won't listen to you. Don't talk to me." Like a child, he put his fingers in his ears.

She leaned still closer and went on reciting her mistreatment by bus drivers and the world, and he sat there with his fingers in his ears, his head trembling as if taken with some terrible fit.

At last she stopped, and they rode in silence the rest of the way to Arlington Cemetery.

In the parking zone, the tour guide gave precise instructions about when to meet him and where, but the choreographer was not listening. She stayed with them only long enough to watch the woman slip her hand into her son's hand and to notice he did not resist. The choreographer hurried to the nearest rest room and retched, again and again. She did not rejoin the tour.

She resolved to put the experience out of her mind. Even as a young girl studying dance she had known how to erase memory—she simply willed it gone—and, with varying success, she had done so ever since. Failure did not exist for her; she erased all memory of it. She sometimes felt she owed her continued triumphs as an artist to this odd ability she had developed.

And so the day was lost forever and she returned to the library. She was at heart an intellectual dancer.

Weeks passed, and months, and every day she went off dutifully to her American research. At times she became depressed, and then she would flirt with the dark temptation to explore her own soul and leave America to itself. But she resisted and went on. She told herself that discovering a dance took talent and time and endless patience, and at sixty-one she had them all, and luck too. She could wait. She would find the true America she needed by looking askance, catching it from the corner of her eye. That is how she always found the truth in her dances: not by looking into them, or behind them, but by accident and from the side.

And that is how it happened. The choreographer was leafing through an encyclopedia of notable American women, not really thinking about what she was doing but just putting in her time, when the name of Lizzie Borden rose up off the page. At once she closed the book, and closed her eyes, and there in the dusty secret library the dance began to create itself, and she let it. She did not interfere. For an eternity the dance unfolded from inside her while she stood and waited. And then she moved on tiptoe around the edges of it, making sure that it was whole and good. She called it *An American Memory*.

It was not at all what she had first intended, she thought. But was anything? Ever?

A GIFT

Prentice was a musician by birth and talent, with nearly perfect pitch and a voice, when he spoke, of such tone and amplitude that people always turned to see who was speaking. The tragedy of his life was that he could not sing.

The tragedy of the moment, however, was that he could not find a damned parking place. He had driven up and down the rows of cars for nearly ten minutes now and there was simply no place to park in the side lot. He could see there were lots of places in the front lot, but that would mean a long walk to Neiman's and he just didn't have the time. He'd find a place here if it killed him. He had come close, but he missed every likely spot. A Mercedes—of course—was parked crooked so that it took up a place and a half. A huge RV took up two. And an old lady, some refugee from Willard Scott, had spent forever getting her packages into the back seat, and then she patted her hair for a while, and when she finally got into the car, she just sat there; perhaps dead. Horns had honked, and Prentice could see a number of cars behind him, so he said to hell with it and hit the accelerator, laying rubber. Cars kept pulling out and other cars kept pulling in, seconds before him. Were the gods telling him something?

He was going to be late for office hours and nothing made him crazier than being late. He always told students they could give him excuses for not knowing a piece and excuses for not playing it well, but there were no excuses, ever, for being late.

Prentice was Chairman of the Music Department. He taught performance techniques, theory, aesthetics, and musical resources of the eighteenth, nineteenth, and twentieth centuries. This is what you do, he told his wife, when you've got everything to succeed as a singer except talent: you teach. So he took teaching very seriously, and administrating just as seriously, and that is why he was driving around the parking lot during his lunch hour. He was going to Neiman's to buy a box of Godiva truffles for his secretary, not because it was National Secretary Week or because she had done some extra work for him, but simply because she was a wonderful secretary and he wanted her to know he appreciated her. Spontaneous gifts were the best gifts. A little noontime surprise, for no reason at all, was part of being the thoughtful administrator. If he couldn't sing, Prentice reasoned, he could at least be perfect in some other way. He could at least be a good man.

Thinking of her pleasure and surprise, he began to feel a little less miserable and, to counter the feeling, he began to sing softly, badly, the Flower Song from *Carmen*. Caught up in the melody, Prentice realized too late that while he dawdled, a woman had pulled ahead of him and would now get the space that would have been his. She stopped to wait for the car to back out so she could pull in. Like it or not, he had to wait behind her. Nothing was happening. No movement at all. Prentice craned his neck to see what was wrong. An old *old* guy was destroying a collapsible stroller that wouldn't collapse for him. He yanked it and pushed it and held it down with one foot while he kicked it with the other, and all this time three little kids were running around him, getting in his way and shrieking like maniacs. The woman ahead of him, who would get the old fart's parking place, just sat there with one arm stretched across the back of the seat, the other dangling loose and relaxed from the car window. She was maddening.

Prentice backed up a little bit, hoping he could pull around her car, but there was not quite enough space on her right and the kids were dancing around *le fart ancien* on her left, so he just gave up and screamed instead. A falsetto scream from *Tosca*. His throat hurt, but the scream had relieved his desire to kill.

The old man finally crammed the stroller into the trunk and the kids into the back seat and went on to torture the rearview mirror and then the seat belts. Finally, without even a glance behind, he backed out with a roar, stopped, looked around to see if he had hit anybody, and then slowly drove away. At last.

But the woman still sat there, one arm sticking out of the window, the other moving slowly, slowly, to the steering wheel. The bitch. Prentice leaned on the horn as hard as he could. Her car had begun moving, but she stopped at the horn blast and turned around to look at him over her shoulder. "Move your goddamned car!" he shouted and, since he knew she couldn't hear him, he shook his clenched fist at her. She smirked at him. He leaned on the horn long and hard. Slowly, infuriatingly, she pulled into his parking space.

Prentice gunned his car, jolting it forward to the end of the row, and made a swift right turn toward the front parking lot. He'd walk the distance to Neiman's and be done with this whole damned business. But instantly he thought how unfair it was, and how enraging, for her to take the moral high ground, giving him a look like that, after she'd stolen his place. Well might *she* be patient. *She* had all day. What did she have to do but shop? She would patter around Nordstrom's for a while, and then the new Macy's with its thousand-dollar price tags, and then she'd hit Neiman's for tea and a croissant, and then home to Atherton to see how cook was getting on with the dinner. His head pounding, Prentice gave the steering wheel a sharp yank to the right, and then another, and tore back to where she'd taken his place. He spotted her just getting out of her car and, at exactly the same moment, he spotted—only five cars down—an empty parking space. He pulled into it, jumped out of his car, and turned to face her. She walked past him, refusing to make eye contact. She was just what he'd thought: rich, elegant, indulged, a bitch.

"You certainly are a courteous driver," he called after her, his voice clotted with rage.

"You!" She rounded on him as if she'd been waiting for this. "You might at least have the decency to wait while an old man puts his grandchildren into the car." She paused and Prentice noticed she had a rich velvety contralto, perfect for her type. "What did you want me to do? Run over them? What kind of man *are* you? You're selfish. Purely selfish."

"Selfish! *I'm* selfish? *You* just sat there, taking the air, sunning yourself until you felt in the mood . . . the old fool already *had* them in the car . . ." He broke off and strode away because his voice was cracking and he was near tears.

". . . think you're the only person in the world. Arrogant. Self-important . . ."

Prentice turned and walked back to her. "You don't know anything about me. You say *I'm* arrogant? *I'm* self-important? After you just sit there, sprawled across the front seat, perfectly aware that you're blocking my way, having *first* taken my parking place, and you knew, you *knew* I was desperate to get around you, and you deliberately took as much time as you could. *You*'ve got all the time in the world, so everybody else can just wait behind you. You think *I'm* inhuman? You make me sick."

He left her then and walked to the end of the row of cars and crossed over to Neiman's. He could hear her behind him, this elegant woman, shouting in her lush contralto, "selfish" and "hateful."

He kept on walking. They were barbarians, both of them, they were uncivilized. No wonder there were wars. No wonder everybody hated everybody else. He stopped for a moment and wiped his mouth. He could taste acid. He wanted to spit. He wanted to throw up. He turned around and walked toward her. She pulled back a little as if he might strike her.

"I'm sorry," he said. "I'm not like this. I apologize."

"You," she said, a lifetime of hatred in the word.

"Listen," he said, choking, urgent. "I apologize. This is no way to act. It's all awful enough. It's unspeakable, life, I mean. And I make it worse by being like this. So I apologize. I'm sorry."

She stared at him, her eyes wide.

"I am," Prentice said. "I'm not like this."

She continued to stare, and then her eyes narrowed, and she said, "Yes, you are." She gave him a smile, not a nice one, and walked past him into Neiman's.

Prentice stared after her and then walked slowly to the entrance. He stood outside for a moment, looking into the store, and then he turned and walked back to his car. He drove, numb and silent, the short distance to campus. He found a parking place at once.

He was drowning in emotion—frustration, anger, jealousy, shame, desire, endless and eternal desire—so instead of going to his office, Prentice walked up two flights of stairs to the rehearsal rooms where somebody was sure to be practicing. He went down the corridor, listening near each door, and then he stopped outside Room 14. He recognized the voice at once. It was Chip Coleman, that pig from L.A. who had a great natural tenor but who never practiced. He was mindless, reckless, and disgusting, but he had a tenor voice of such purity and range that Prentice forgave him everything. He was practicing "Cielo e Mar" from *La Gioconda*. He had his breathing nicely under control, and as he caressed the melodic line, his voice was strong and clear. He hit a clinker, but recovered at once and went on with ease and confidence. Prentice listened as the pig came to the most difficult passage, but his miraculous voice soared effortlessly above A to that impossible high B, which he hit and held, a long and pure expression of human yearning and desire. If there were indeed a heavenly choir, this is how it would sound.

Anyone passing in the corridor at that moment would have seen the Chairman of the Department leaning hard against the door of Practice Room 14, his head bowed as he concentrated on the music. He might have appeared to be crying, though he made no sound, and in fact the expression on his face was inscrutable: erotic or murderous, who could say?

He turned from the voice at last and, with a new awareness on his face, he started downstairs to his office, telling himself that surely he could get through one more afternoon, and then perhaps the next, and the next.

NIGHTFALL

That summer during the late evenings and the cold endless nights that followed, young girls all over West Hadley lay awake hoping to hear the sounds of Rory O'Toole.
The screech of his tires, the thunder of his terrible motor,
and those girls turned luxuriously in their beds, knowing that
at last Rory was laying rubber in their street.

Rory was an artist of the motorcycle and he was a female
disturbance also, and Rebecca's mother said he was a disease.
A pestilence. He was eighteen or maybe twenty-eight or
thirty, with a heavy blond beard and low jeans. Rory was
from Australia, however, and so at first the police and then

later just about everybody realized it wasn't his fault, this female hysteria he excited. Nonetheless, he did excite it. Nonetheless, all those young girls were lying awake in hope and expectation. Nonetheless, he was to blame.

Rory's motorcycle was a Honda 750, with no extra chrome and no options, but he rode it as if it had once been wild, and he had roped and tamed it himself, and now it idled or roared or reared between his legs like some savage thing that he had made his own. His, only.

Rory was an incident. He was an occasion. Rory, Rebecca's mother kept saying, was a disease. Rebecca and her mother both—but each in her own way—were victims of this disease.

.　　.　　.

Rebecca's mother had been modern for a long time. She realized that they were living in the 1990s and so there was no chance of her Rebecca's being ruined. Ruin had stopped in the 1970s. Now all the girls—even the ones in West Hadley—had large breasts by the age of twelve, and they had experience too. They were sophisticated about safe sex and motorcycles and diseases. Rebecca's mother knew all this and did not really worry about Rebecca's possible ruin, but still she wanted something done about Rory, and she decided to get it done through the town Selectmen. Her husband was a Selectman, and even though he was personally useless to her, at least he was a contact. She could get what she wanted.

The Selectmen of West Hadley also wanted something done about Rory, even if he was an Australian and couldn't help it. The Selectmen were not concerned about ruin any more than Rebecca's mother was; they were concerned about water pollution, about sleeping nights, about getting that goddamn motorcycle off the side roads and onto the highway straight out of town. Who cares who screws who? Or what? Or why? Let's get some sleep, for Chrissake, let's at least have some relaxation, could we only just watch "The Tonight Show" in peace?

.　.　.

Rebecca's mother sat alone with her pitcher of late-night martinis and said to the test pattern on the television: "Enough is enough. Rory O'Toole goes, or I go. And I'm not going." Too many nights now Rory's laid rubber and the peeling out of that infernal machine had awakened her to Johnny talking away, or David Letterman, or—worst of all— to a flickering test pattern, her martini clutched upright and in perfect balance, her mind fixed on Rory O'Toole. It was not that motorcycle thing he drove—the blatancy of it, the cheap sex of it—that wasn't what sickened her. It was . . . well, what was it? She put down her glass and headed for the stairs.

Let's face it. This is home. This is normal. This is a small New England town where there are no suicides and practically no murders. And who in hell is this Rory O'Toole that he can get away with terrorizing our children, destroying family life, et cetera, et cetera? There *has* to be a moral perspective on all this.

Thus she made it up the stairs and could go to bed. But first she looked in on Rebecca, who was twelve, going on thirteen, and who had fine large breasts, larger than her own. Rebecca was smiling toward the window, toward the last explosions of Rory's Honda 750. She ignored her mother, that drunk at the door.

"Rebecca," the mother said. "Forget him, this Rory. He's no good for you, sweetheart. He's my age. He's your mother's age."

"Go away," Rebecca said.

"Rebecca, my baby."

"Bug off," Rebecca said, still turned to the window.

There was silence for a moment.

"Let me tell you, kid," Rebecca's mother said, shifting gears. "In the showdown, either he goes or I go. And I'm not going."

"Look," Rebecca said, and she placed her pudgy hands firmly beneath her splendid breasts. "See?"

The mother looked as if she did not quite understand.

"In the showdown," Rebecca said, "*you'll* go."

. . .

Rory was coming for dinner and they were all going to get a chance to see him up close. At first Rebecca's mother didn't want him to come on that night because she had insisted that her husband bring home three town Selectmen and their wives. The cream of West Hadley, and Rory? No, it was impossible.

"Not in my home, Rebecca," she said. "Not for dinner. At least not tonight."

"He's coming. I asked him to come and he's coming."

"Rebecca, be reasonable. I'm your mother. You're only twelve."

"Going on thirteen."

"You're only twelve going on thirteen and he can't come here tonight. Not tonight, darling. Tonight is special. Look, I'm not even having a drink. For the company."

Rebecca looked at her with narrowed eyes.

"Let him come tomorrow night and he can have dinner, and if you want, he can stay over. You can sleep in the tent in the backyard. Okay? All right? Or you can have our room, the water bed. But I don't want him in your room, darling. It's not right. I'm a mother."

"The things you say. If the Selectmen only knew."

"It's the Selectmen who want him out of town, Rebecca. He's an influence, Rebecca. He's disruptive. None of the girls are sleeping. It's his motorcycle, Rebecca. It's what it *means*."

"If West Hadley knew about you."

"Well, then, let him come. I'm through with arguing. I'm through with trying to be the sensible one. Let the Selectmen see him up close, with his beard and that big thing. It's just a shame that it has to happen in my house."

And so Rory was coming for dinner.

.   .   .

The Selectmen and their wives drank a lot before dinner, nervous at the prospect of finally meeting the legendary Rory. Rebecca passed chips and onion dip among the eight people, and everybody smiled at her and complimented her on her big breasts, but clearly their thoughts were elsewhere. Rebecca's mother said nothing and drank nothing. This was probably the best thing after all: Rory would condemn himself simply by being what he was. She could take satisfaction in having set everything in motion.

Rory arrived as they were about to sit down to dinner. There was a lot of talk about food and acid rain and air pollution and then they got down to business.

"So you're the famous Mr. O'Toole."

"Right."

"More of the roast, Mr. O'Toole?" That was Rebecca's mother.

"No."

"Rebecca?"

"No."

"Well, well. Mr. O'Toole of the motorcycle and the midnight rides."

"Right."

"The Mr. O'Toole who has all our young girls awake nights and . . . how shall I say it . . . palpitating!"

"It's my Honda 750."

"More broccoli, Mr. O'Toole? Rebecca?" The mother again.

"No."

"No."

"Do you plan to be working here in West Hadley for long, Mr. O'Toole?"

"I don't work."

"Ah. Well, then, you'll probably be moving on before long. Is that right?"

"Maybe. Maybe not."

"We'd be interested to give you a hand, to help you move on, Mr. O'Toole. If, as Selectmen, there is any way we could help?"

"More rolls?" Mother.

"Stuff those rolls."

"*Any* way we might help."

"Enough is enough. I want a martini." Rebecca's mother got up and went to the sideboard where she poured straight gin into a tumbler and then returned to the table. "I'm making up," she said. "Enough is enough."

For a long time nobody said anything and then Rory spoke in his thin caressing voice. "I like to drive my bike," he said. "I like to drive late at night up and down the side roads where all those middle-class birds live, the hot ones, around twelve or thirteen years old, and I rev my engine—get it?—and I sit way back, way back, and I bust through all that air that's out in front of me, blocking my way, and then I'm free, man, free."

"If as Selectmen we could help?"

"You're old," Rory said caressingly. "You're dead men and you don't know it." He looked significantly at Rebecca and Rebecca's mother and the wives of the three Selectmen. They looked back at him, fatally. Then he said, "They know. They want what I've got."

Someone cleared his throat.

"And I'm going to give it to them. I'm going to ride my bike and I'm going to take your women with me. All of them. They know what I've got."

"Have you no moral sense *at all,* Mr. O'Toole?"

"I'm just the temptation." He was purring. "You better look somewhere else for a moral sense." He ran his smile over the women.

Slowly then, Rory O'Toole got up and took Rebecca's hand and led her to the front door.

"You can't leave," Rebecca's mother said through her martini. "I forbid you to go."

"I'm not going," Rebecca said at the door. "And Rory's not going." She placed her hands beneath those infuriating breasts. "You're the one that's going."

.   .   .

A week passed. Every night Rebecca left the house at eleven and returned, exhausted, at three. Every night her midnight cries and the explosions of Rory's motorcycle echoed in the streets of West Hadley. Rebecca's mother could endure it no longer. She woke Rebecca at five one morning, her glittering eyes holding the child awake.

"What is it like, Rebecca? Tell me. Tell me what he's got."

Rebecca gazed at her mother emptily for a moment and then said, "Listen to old raisin tits," and she turned to face the wall.

.   .   .

Enough is enough, Rebecca's mother had said, and it was. The Selectmen talked a lot to one another about Rory O'Toole and, in secret, about their wives, and then they talked to the police. There were laws to be observed, the

Selectmen pointed out, not least of all the laws of proportion, and the police would simply have to do something. Rebecca was out every night roaring around town with that maniac, and Rebecca's mother was all upset, and who could tell who would be next? Besides, that is what police were for. To do something. Still, there was some worry and a lot of talk around the stationhouse after they finally did it.

"But you're sure you got rid of him?"

"We beat him up. We kicked the shit out of him."

"But will he bring charges?"

"How can he? We're the police."

"Well, I hope it all looks clean."

"Looks clean? It is clean. This is West Hadley, for Chrissake. This is a normal New England town. We're just protecting our kids."

"What about the girl with him, that Rebecca? Is she going to be all right?"

"Well, that's a problem. That's a real problem. She's what you call a casualty. Her head got in the way, is what, but she'll be all right where she is. She'll never know the difference. Not at that place. They're all the same there, veggies, except most of them got born that way."

"Some knockers on that kid, that Rebecca."

"Not really. Thirty-eights. That's normal. She's almost thirteen years old."

"So long as O'Toole is gone, that's what matters."

"We did it for our kids. We did it for our women."

"He brought out the worst in people, that O'Toole."

"Well, he's a goner now."

．　　．　　．

But Rory was not gone. His jaw was broken in three places and all his front teeth had been knocked out by the tire iron across his face. One eye was damaged. And seven ribs were cracked. But his groin, despite the heavy boots of the police, remained perfectly intact.

He mended. He got well. Rebecca's mother, who had wanted it all to happen, who had invited the Selectmen to put pressure on the police, felt bad about it now and brought him flowers and homemade soup. She brought him martinis. She brought him photographs of herself as a girl at the beach, playing tennis, graduating from college. She touched the poor sore jaw, and his hurt ribs, and she moved her hand down beneath the covers. She liked to visit hospitals; and God knows there was no point in visiting Rebecca.

Within a month Rory was out and on his Honda 750, with his beard and his low jeans and a stunning leather patch over one eye. The police had decided on a hands-off policy because of the Rebecca incident, and the town Selectmen felt bad too.

And so that autumn during the evenings and into the late cold nights that followed, Rebecca's mother and Rory O'Toole shattered the frosty silence of West Hadley as they tore through the side roads and up the expansive hills, laying rubber. At the sound of their going, the wives of Selectmen throughout the town turned luxuriously in their beds, smiling to themselves, certain that their life was good, their fate inescapable.

REJOICE AND BE GLAD

Janet had been dying for two months now from the uterine cancer she'd had for a year. She knew the whole time it was growing in her womb that it was indeed that unspeakable thing, but once her doctor had mumbled the fatal word, cancer, it grew wildly, terminally, as if in naming it, he gave it the power to kill.

Janet had slammed her way through life, independent, self-sufficient, and she was damned if cancer was going to change any of that. She would be honest and forthright. She would live with it. Since she had no husband, she told her friends she had cancer, period, and she intended to treat it as merely

67

part of her life, not the end of it. She was fifty-five, her own woman, and she would tough it out. But her friends could not bear all this bravery and positive thinking, and after a first visit, and for some a second, they had fallen away—no one needed this memento mori—and now they no longer even phoned. Her pride and her courage, as much as her coming death, had driven them off.

Janet would die early in the new year. She knew that. And now, with only weeks to go, perhaps only days, she had begun to regret her courage and her pride and would have settled for a little sympathy. Pity, even, on a day like this one. She would have liked to tell somebody she was nearly dead and have them say "Oh no!" and have them touch her and say they cared, once, before the end. Was it so bad to want a human word? A touch?

She brooded on this every day, and much of the night, and she was brooding on it now as she stood at the upstairs window watching the wind blow the light snow in soft eddies, waiting for the cancer to finish its work. She looked away from the window at the clock on the dresser—it was getting late—and when she turned back to the window she saw a boy trudging through the snow to the house across the road. Where had he come from? No one was home over there and so he continued trudging on to the next door. Now he was standing in the road looking at her house. It was the day before Christmas and nobody in the neighborhood was home, except Janet, who was always home. Watching him out there, with his scarf and his blond hair blowing in the wind, she had this crazy thought: if he rang her bell, it would be a sign. She would let him in, and she would tell him, and he would say "Oh no!" and touch her, maybe.

But he seemed undecided. He looked up and down the road. He looked at his watch. He scratched his behind for a moment while he made his decision and then he started up to her door.

She let the bell ring three times before she answered it. It couldn't really be a sign. She must be crazy.

"What?" she said, holding the door open an inch or two.

"Rejoice and be glad, for today is born to you a Savior! Glory to God in the highest! And on earth, peace to men of good will!" He paused for breath. "Be not afraid, for behold I bring you good news of great joy which will come to all the people. . . ."

"What're you? Nuts?" She used her tough voice.

"Hi," he said. "Merry Christmas."

It was a standoff and she knew it. She was a dying woman of fifty-five, half crazy with pain and loneliness, and he was— what? fourteen or fifteen?—with ignorant Christian joy written all over his pink and yellow face. Somebody was going to have to give.

"Nobody comes here," she said, holding the door just wide enough for him to squeeze through. "Nobody gets in." An icy blast came in with the boy, filling the entryway with cold air and the smell of cinnamon. She pulled her flannel housecoat tight around her. "So what do you want?"

"The lion will lie down with the lamb."

"Cut that crap," she said.

He looked around the entryway and then he looked into the little living room and then he looked at Janet. His eyes were night blue and large, concealing nothing. He grinned at her.

"What?" she said.

"You let me in," he said.

"I don't let people in,"she said. "There hasn't been anybody in here in twenty-seven days, not even the gas man. I wouldn't let him read the meter. I don't see anybody and I don't talk to anybody."

He took one step into the living room and looked around. No Christmas tree, no decorations. Just an old sofa and a couple of chairs and a TV. On top of the TV there was a bunch of photographs, graduation pictures, mostly women.

"These your kids?" he said.

"Friends," she said. "They're all dead now."

The boy shrugged and stepped back into the entryway. He grinned once more and rubbed his hands together.

"Do you want a cup of coffee?"

"I want some booze. You got whiskey?"

"It's only instant. I can't be bothered with percolating."

"Haven't you even got a beer?"

"How old are you, anyway?"

"Fourteen or fifteen, I guess. I guess I'm fourteen."

"I'll make you coffee," Janet said.

. . .

The boy was sitting at the kitchen table and Janet was standing at the stove, her arms folded across her breasts, waiting for the water to boil. Neither said anything. There was a buzzing sound in the room from the electric clock and they heard a snowplow go by in the street. Janet looked at him. Was he the one she could tell?

"You didn't take off your overshoes and now there's a puddle on my floor," she said.

"Oh," the boy said.

She turned back to the saucepan, where the water had finally begun to bubble. "Kids don't care," she said. She made the coffee and brought the cups to the table. She sat down opposite him.

"So. What're you selling?"

"Me? What'm I selling? I'm not selling anything. I'm straight."

"Then what's all this glad tidings of great joy stuff?"

He burned his lip on the coffee. "I usually take milk," he said.

"So do I," she said. "I'm out. So what're you selling?"

He took a funny-looking cigarette from his pocket, licked it expertly and, with a grin in Janet's direction, he struck a match and lit up. He inhaled, holding the smoke in his lungs for a long moment, and then slowly, languorously, he let the smoke slip from between his thin lips. He smiled without showing his teeth.

"Marijuana," she said.

"It's good," he said. "You should try it."

Janet stared at him for a while as if she might take him up on his offer, but then she took another sip of coffee instead.

"So, what're you selling?" she said.

"Candy bars," he said. He inhaled again, drawing the smoke deep into his lungs, concentrating. When he had exhaled, he slumped a little, getting comfortable, leaning his head against the hard rail of the chair. "Mmmmm," he said.

"That stuff'll kill you," she said. "Excuse me." She got up and went to the foot of the stairs. "Don't take anything," she said. After a long while the toilet flushed and she came downstairs again. "You didn't take anything," she said, half a question, looking around the kitchen

The boy was seated exactly where she had left him. A little smile was playing on his lips.

"I took the stove," he said. "I've got it in my pocket." He giggled.

"That stuff has made you silly," she said. She fixed herself another cup of coffee.

The boy sat there, silent, and Janet sat opposite him, hunched over her coffee cup. The company was nice. It was reassuring. He said nothing and she said nothing, and after a while she forgot he was there. Her face went blank and her eyes emptied, her half-crazy look. She had gone away to wherever it was she went when she looked into her future. The boy's cigarette burned down to nothing and their coffee went cold, and still they sat there like this.

. . .

"Oh, wow," the boy said. He shook his head several times. "Far out. Right?"

And so Janet, too, came back.

"Rejoice and be glad," he said, still shaking his head.

"What do you want here?" she said. Her mood had changed.

"Oh, man!"

"It's getting late," she said.

"I could really use, like, something to eat. I mean I've got the bad munchies." He rubbed his eyes, hard, as if he were trying to gouge them out. "Weed does that to you; it puts you away real nice."

"Puts you away," she said.

"And then afterward you want to eat and you want to talk. At least I do. It's great. You got something to eat?"

Janet put saltines on a plate and brought them to the table. "That's it," she said, and watched as he ate the saltines one after another, ravenously, until the plate was empty.

"You better go now," she said. "What're you doing here anyhow? You're not from around here."

"No," the boy said.

"Well, what're you, a thief?"

"No, I told you. I'm straight." He grinned, and looked at her frankly, openly. "I used to hustle," he said, "but I do this now, mostly. Sell candy bars for five bucks. It's like symbolic. I tell people the profits go to a youth program for drug rehab, and it's true in a way, because I used to be on the heavy stuff and now I only do grass. There are a bunch of us. Lenny drops us off in the likely places and then he picks us up in a couple hours and we all split the profits. Lenny used to hustle too."

"This is what you call straight? If you were my . . ." but she left the words unfinished.

"It beats being on the street. Well, to tell you the truth, I'd still be on the street, except I'm not young enough anymore. The old guys want you real young, if you get me. Maybe I'll go back later, I don't know. This is good right now. You know?"

He was looking into her eyes, and she returned his look. She was trying to say something, but she had no words for it, and after a moment the boy lowered his glance. They sat there, silent. He cleared his throat. He fiddled with his scarf. Finally he looked at his watch, and said, "I'd better go. Lenny'll be cruising out there, looking for me." He seemed to want to reassure her. "There's nothing to worry about. Lenny's real good to us, you know? He's the one teaches us the Bible verses. He was, like, in a born-again seminary even before he was a hustler."

"You have your whole life ahead of you," she said, ferocious suddenly. "You've gotta be tough. You can't depend on people to take care of you, to live your life for you. I was tough all my life. I was my own person." She stopped and looked at him for a moment. "No," she said. "Don't listen to me. Let me tell you what I want from you. I want . . ." But she only stared ahead into her future.

"Yeah, well," he said. "Thanks for the coffee." He took a large Hershey bar from his pocket and slipped it onto the table. "I'd like to give you this, free, okay? Like, for Christmas."

Janet reached out and touched the candy bar. And then she took it in her hands and for a second it seemed she was going to press it to her chest. But she just put it back on the table, one hand resting on it.

The boy stood up and looked out the window toward the street. "I think I see Lenny's car," he said. "He's cruising."

Still Janet said nothing.

"Well," he said, "Glory to God in the highest and all that stuff." He grinned at her. "Okay," he said.

He pulled his scarf tight around his neck and knotted it. "See you," he said. He was in the entryway, about to open the door. "Okay," he said again.

Janet stood behind him, the Hershey bar clutched in her right hand. With her left she pointed at the photographs on top of the television. "They aren't dead," she said. "They're my friends. I'm the one that's dying."

The boy opened the door and stepped outside. "Wow, it's cold," he said.

"Cancer," she said. "I've only got days. I want you to touch me. I want to give you a kiss."

"Hey, Lenny!" he shouted. He waved at an old Ford and took off down the stairs. "Lenny!"

"It's all right," Janet said, standing at the open door. "It's all right." She watched the Ford come to a stop and wait for the boy. The car was filled with kids. She could hear them laughing even from her doorstep. She was still standing there, the Hershey bar in her hand, as the car drove away.

THEMSELVES

Harriet and Margaret. Margaret and Harriet. Oh, *there* were two. Wide-winged and passionate, they swooped down on a banquet table like goddesses of chaos, turning conversations inside out, exposing fools, worshiping folly, whipping up an intellectual revolution. *You* know. There they were; and utterly at home in any dining room anywhere, in Paris at the George V or in some rundown apartment in east L.A. *Chez eux*, wherever they happened to be. Themselves.

When I knew them, they were in their seventies. Beautiful still, with those fine bones and the inner calm that comes from knowing right at the start that you belong, you have a place in it all. But deep beneath the inner calm lay something else, something fine and problematic, but that doesn't come in until later. So.

Margaret and Harriet. Margaret first.

Margaret had no fear, but quite a bit of craziness. It was Margaret who decided one night that she was in love with the man next door and right away, dressed only in her nightgown, she went and stood on his lawn in the moonlight, waiting for him to look out and see her there. She knew that this was crazy. They were both in their forties at the time and she already had a perfectly good husband. Nonetheless she had decided that this was the great passion of her middle life and she'd be a fool not to risk everything for passion, so she did. Every night for two weeks, then, she stood out there on the lawn, risking pneumonia, risking discovery by the neighbor's wife, risking arrest when you think of it. The pneumonia got her first and, after that, she decided she wasn't interested in this neighbor after all. Also, she liked to stand up in canoes, she drank the water in Mexico, and she refused to comprehend money. And she always, whatever the situation, said what she was thinking.

There are other examples of Margaret's folly, as you can imagine from what you know already.

Now for Harriet. Harriet had some fear, and a little craziness, but no folly at all. Harriet was afraid of offending anybody except mean people. She was afraid of other people dying, because she had known about her brother and her other sister before they died, and she knew about Margaret. There was nothing she could alter about other people dying and *that* was why she was afraid of *that*. Of her own dying she was less afraid; still, she didn't like the idea of not being, and she didn't like the process, because it would be such a mess disintegrating in front of people who had known her whole. But she wasn't afraid of spiders or giving a speech or rapers and murderers or entering a strange room full of people or any of the ordinary things. Moreover, her craziness was merely verbal, no baying at the moon for Harriet, and her folly was nonexistent.

What Harriet and Margaret had in common was this: they were sisters and they were dervishes. They spun. They were a fire storm in the living room.

That's how it was when they had dinner at my place the night I died.

What Harriet and Margaret have in common now is: me.

Well, get on with it. The dinner, as I've said, was my last. Ron was there, and Stephanie and Michael, P. Fish of course, and *moi*. They all arrived in a bunch and then, before they even had drinks in their hands, in came Harriet and Margaret. Talking and laughing and taking off coats and handing around drinks: that's how it was. "What a wonderful apartment, I've never seen so many books, how do you keep it so nice." And so forth. Margaret and Harriet, Harriet and Margaret, making a party. "What a delicious dinner, I think this is the best dinner I've ever had in my life." But you've all been to busy dinners, so you know.

And, in fact, I didn't really have that many books and the dinner was just J. J. and F.'s chicken cordon bleu that I bought already layered and rolled and tucked up and then just heated in my oven, but it was nice in the roar of the fire storm to hear such a generous acknowledgment of my efforts. Nobody mentioned the flowers, it's true, but then again the flowers had already put on a wilty look before anybody arrived. False economy. Be advised.

But none of this is the point. The point is that Margaret was gaggling away, being a party, with her life already hostage to cancer and with the promise of a year at most. And Harriet too, because she was seventy-something and frenzied with too much caring and too much being responsible for the world, dear kind mad Harriet, the dervish of Dartmouth Street, *she* must have known what lay around the next dark corner. I, however, was the only one to go. Death had been ticking in my head for such a long time and I had never heard it. And then, ping! after the guests had gone but before I even finished washing the dishes, I had the stroke, and my brain simply burst with the effort of accommodating all the new things that were going on, and, well, here I am.

But really that is not the point either. The point is the conversation we had. Margaret, like everybody, is an atheist, but like all atheists she's fascinated that some people believe in God. She can't imagine why. So she asks them all the time. In this crowd, Ron and I are Catholics of a sort, Stephanie was married to a Catholic once, and Michael was raised a Catholic but he doesn't care for Catholicism anymore. I should add that I used to be a priest and now I'm not. Or rather, to be absolutely accurate, I am still a priest—because you can't stop being a priest any more than you can stop being a Christian or a Jew—but I don't do priest things any longer. So, with a crowd like this, it was inevitable that Margaret would ask lots of questions, and she did, and so there were lots of answers.

But mostly she wanted to know *how* I could believe, and I tried to explain that faith isn't something you choose, it's something you're given, except that in a way you have to *want* to choose it. But how can you want it, Margaret said, if you don't even know what it is. In fact *why* would you want it? Well, it's all too confusing, and she was done with it, she thought.

Well, it *was* confusing because right across the table Stephanie was telling Ron and P. Fish how she married her first husband in a Catholic ceremony on a beach in Hawaii, but it was all perfectly legal even though it was exotic, and P. Fish was saying he'd had no idea Catholics were so broad-minded, and Ron was trying to say they weren't and they shouldn't be and that Stephanie was undoubtedly mistaken in thinking it was a *Roman* Catholic ceremony, it was probably something else. Harriet volunteered to the Stephanie conversation that she preferred Catholics to Baptists because the Catholics at least promised you something in the next life even if it might only be hell, whereas the Baptists didn't promise you anything here or there. And she volunteered to the Margaret conversation that faith was impossible because you couldn't believe in what you didn't know about, and what you did know about was so appalling that it was better not to even think of it, and anyhow did I prefer Jesus to God? Or who? And why did Catholics have to have so *many?*

So many Gods? I tried to change the subject to poor nations or to folly or fear, to just anything, but Margaret would not let go of the question of faith and Harriet kept wanting to know faith in *whom?* or in *what?* And then they moved on to grace, or rather Harriet did, because she kept hearing about grace in Flannery O'Connor, and had never been able to figure out what it was. And so once again I tried to explain. "Oh, I see," Harriet said at last, "grace is just exactly like nothing . . . except it hurts."

Well, what was the use. I cleared away the dishes and brought out the fruit and Brie and lots more wine. The noise level continued to rise, and the fun, and all of a sudden Margaret just sort of wailed, "Oh, I'm so tired of Jesus and God."

And that's how we got to where we are now. Something happened in my skull then, factually as well as figuratively, and though I didn't realize it, at that moment the definitive step had been taken: for Margaret, for Harriet, for me.

This is the point: God is absolutely ironic. When you hear someone say, But why *me?* How could God let this happen to *me?* you can be sure you are listening to a person who doesn't know about irony. And when you read in the *Enquirer* about how some desirable actress withered away and died of sheer loneliness, or when you read in the *Lives of the Saints* that somebody who was proud got the pride kicked out of him before he could become a saint, or when you're dead and comfortable and can look into secret hearts and discover that the only way God can get to some people is by treating them to a good long look at their alcoholism or by helping them to discover beneath their arrogant defensive armor of virility, guess what? yes, the thin strong thread of homosexuality, well, to round this out and wrap it up, when you see somebody destroyed by his virtues and, ironically, rescued by his weaknesses or what he thinks are weaknesses, then you see the point about irony. Except that with God, as you know, irony is absolute.

So there we were at the dinner table, all of us tired of God and Jesus, but especially Margaret and Harriet, who were not used to giving either of them that much time, when something happened in my skull, a tick so quiet I didn't even notice, just God calling. The definitive step had been taken. Oh Margaret. Oh Harriet.

Then there were exclamations, how late it is, what a wonderful dinner, everyone deranged and interesting, and finally the coats and kisses and goodbye.

Goodbye. Goodbye.

Before I'd even closed the door, death slipped into my life, barely breathing, tenebrous, loitering beside me while I rinsed glasses and sorted silverware and put the dishes in the sink.

In good time, it was over. A bloody flower bloomed inside my head and my eyes seemed to want to get out and all I could think of was Harriet and Margaret, obsessed by other people's faith, besieged by grace, not wanting—they thought—what they could not know. The flower bloomed, and burst, and faded.

Irony is absolute and faith is absolute. And so I go now, all ways, with Harriet and Margaret, trailing in the wake of their laughter and perfume, noting fear, noting folly, noting how all things labor unto good.

Harriet and Margaret. Margaret and Harriet. Oh!

MUTTI

The eight o'clock bell had already rung, but Anton stood on the footbridge anyway, watching the dark water. The bridge was off limits during school hours, but nobody was around to see him now, and Anton liked the feeling he got leaning over the bridge, and so he stood there, waiting. It was cold, and getting colder, but there was no ice on the stream yet. There would be ice on the way home though.

A boy in the lower school had drowned in the stream a year ago; that was why the bridge was off limits.

Anton watched a patch of leaves pull away from the bank and eddy out into the middle of the stream. He squinted,

83

turning the leaves into a brown jacket, his own, floating toward him as he stood above, watching. There was a small rock directly beneath where he stood. If he could make the leaves float toward the rock, touch it, he would have the picture of his own dead body, face down, floating there beneath him. Drowned. He concentrated hard, willing the patch of leaves to drift toward him. But the leaves caught for a moment against a branch and spun in a full circle, trailing behind them a dark green patch, slimy, changing the shape of everything. Then suddenly, for no reason, the leaves broke free of the branch and came to rest against a rock. Anton smiled. Perfect. The back of his head was just visible above the water, the dark brown jacket moved in the stream, washed by it, softly, easily, and Anton inhaled the cold water deeply. Drowned. Dead.

He could not leave the bridge so long as his body lay there in the stream. It was getting late. He always missed the eight o'clock bell, but he did not want to miss the eight-ten and the end of homeroom period. It was Friday, and if Mr. Hollister were to call him in again, it would be today. If he called him in, he would skip gym. If he called him in, he would get through the morning all right, and then maybe the afternoon. And then there would be the stones, and his mother, and all Saturday and Sunday with nothing to be afraid of.

Move, then, he wanted to say to the body beneath the bridge. At once the leaves broke away from the rock. Again Anton smiled. It was going to be a safe day.

.   .   .

In the corridor outside homeroom everything was silent. He peeked through the little glass window and saw Miss Kelly pacing up and down in front of the room. She was wearing her Friday sweater, green-blue and baggy, and she was mopping her nose with a tissue. She always had a cold.

The principal was making the morning announcements and

his muffled voice came in little spurts through the heavy door: PTA, cheerleading, speech club. Anton opened his locker and put away all his books except American history; he would need that for first period. He hung up his coat, his cap, his scarf. He looked both ways for a moment and then quickly, in a single hurried motion, he took off his face and hung it on the side hook, so that only his profile showed. And then he slammed the locker door, ready, as the eight-ten bell rang for first period.

. . .

"You're late, Anton," Miss Kelly said at the classroom door. "Go to the office and get a pass. Oh, and here's a note. Mr. Hollister wants to see you in the Guidance Office during your first free period. So please don't be late for him. You're always late, Anton. I don't know why that has to be." Miss Kelly hugged herself in her green-blue sweater. "Can you tell me why that has to be? That you're always late?"

Anton said nothing.

"Well, I've had a little talk with Mr. Hollister about you. I've told him you're doing very well in English, your written work, but you don't talk enough. You don't contribute. Don't you think you could contribute more?"

Students had begun to drift in for Miss Kelly's English class and some of them were listening, Anton knew.

"We both like you, Anton. Mr. Hollister and I, both. I want you to understand that. We're just concerned about you. You're just so . . ."

But Anton was not listening to her. He was listening to the fat girl in the front row, who was saying to her girlfriend, "We're concerned about you, Anton. We love you, Anton. We adore you. Oh, Anton!"

"Very well," Miss Kelly said, seeing that he was not listening to her, seeing his face redden. "Please see Mr. Hollister during study. And *please* be on time." Brisk now, all business, she said to the class, "All right, people, please settle down. We are still on Chaucer and it is already December and we are a full century behind."

Miss Kelly was in love with Mr. Hollister, Anton knew, and he knew too that Mr. Hollister would never return her love. Mr. Hollister loved him.

. . .

He got through American history and algebra and art without having to say anything. As always, he knew the answers, but he kept silent even when he was called on. He preferred that the others think him stupid and just ignore him. He didn't want them to look at him or talk to him or even talk about him. He wanted not to exist. Or to be invisible. To escape. So he waited.

Even in art class he waited. Art was an elective and Miss Belekis had seen at once that he had a real gift for drafts-manship, so she had loaned him books on anatomy and told him to draw whatever he wanted. She had praised his first drawings—fat peasant women knitting or praying or peeling apples, imitative stuff—and he had liked her praise, but he saw the danger of being noticed. And so for Miss Belekis he drew the same peasant women again and again, trying to make the drawings seem less finished each time, trying to conceal his growing mastery of craft. After a while, he just gave her the same old drawings. She stopped commenting, but she continued to loan him the books.

Years later, as a famous sculptor working in marble and stone, he would remain just as secretive, a mystery to his agent and the galleries where he showed. He was a recluse. He saw almost nobody. And though he always sculpted from life and, in time, went through three wives and a mistress, he claimed he just didn't like people. He merely sculpted them from stone.

But now, in high school, he had no choice. He was forced

to see people. Still, he could keep them from seeing him. And so, though he continued to take home the books that Miss Belekis loaned him, he showed her only the same old pictures of the peasant women. Meanwhile, at nights and on weekends, he made good progress with the human figure, drawing it over and over in every imaginable posture, and always nude. This did not embarrass him. This was art, and it had nothing to do with life.

In life, he was terrified at the idea of a nude body. This was why he cut gym class repeatedly. All the boys taking off their clothes in front of each other, looking, some of them even wanting to be looked at. And Coach Landry encouraging it all. It made him want to run and hide. And they looked at him, too.

Only last night he had been drying himself after his shower when he noticed a few dark brown hairs, down there, and he realized he would never be safe again. He squatted on the bath mat and covered himself with both hands, squeezing tight, and praying "Oh no, God, please don't let me get big there, and have hair that shows, and be like the others. Please don't let me ever be a man." But even as he prayed, he knew it was hopeless. He took his hands away and the dark hairs were still there. It would happen to him, too. Nothing would stop it. Not prayer. Not anything.

. . .

"Anton, my friend. Come right in," Mr. Hollister said. "Have a seat. Go on, sit down. Now tell me. How are things going? Things going okay?"

"Yes." Anton looked down. Mr. Hollister was wearing his red turtleneck. His blond hair was long and floppy. He crossed his legs wrong.

"Good. Good. So how are you doing? Oh, well, we've done that, haven't we. What I really mean, Anton, is that as your guidance counselor I'm concerned about you. I mean, you're

a really bright young man, but you're always late for everything, and your teachers say you don't contribute in class,
and, gosh, I've noticed myself that you're, well, you're . . .
let's say independent. Some might say a loner. Some might
even say antisocial. But I understand that. I do. I was a private
kid myself. Like you, in a way. You know?"

Anton looked up at him and resolved to tell him nothing.
He would break in. He would destroy.

"You're thin, Anton. Do you eat enough? I mean, do you
have a good appetite?"

"Yes."

"Good. Good. Well, frankly, what I really want to ask
about, express my concern about is . . . the bruises. The cuts
on your hands, your face sometimes, that broken wrist you
had. I mean, Anton, how do you have so many accidents, for
instance? I wonder if you could tell me about that."

"I'm clumsy. I'm not careful."

"Well, Anton, I was wondering about your folks. Your
mom and dad. Do you get along with them okay? I mean,
they never hit you or anything, do they?"

"No."

"I mean, those bruises aren't from them. Your father
doesn't hit you or anything? Even once in a while? You could
tell me, you know. I could make sure he'd never hurt you
again."

"He never hits me."

"No, of course not. We just have to check, you know. And
your mother, neither? No?"

"No."

"Well, let's see. I know quite a lot about you," Mr. Hollister
said, and flipped open a manila folder on his desk. "We know
quite a lot about each other, I mean." He leafed through
several sheets of paper.

What he knew was that Anton was fourteen, an only child, male. He was born a United States citizen, of Russian and German parents. His father was a translator of Slavic literature. His mother was a housewife. They had lived in this small Massachusetts town for less than a year. What he knew was that Anton was alone.

"Don't we," Mr. Hollister said.

"Don't we what?"

"We know quite a lot about each other, I mean."

Anton waited for a moment and then looked him full in the eyes. "Yes," he said.

Mr. Hollister cleared his throat and uncrossed his legs and looked again at the sheets of paper in the folder. Slowly his face began to color. When he raised his eyes, he found Anton still looking at him, waiting. He lowered them again.

"Well, anytime you want to talk, Anton, you feel free to just come in here and see me." His voice was different now. "I'm concerned about you, as you know; about all the kids. So you just come ahead anytime. Okay?"

"Thank you," Anton said. He lowered his eyes finally, and then he stood up to go.

"Anytime," Mr. Hollister said.

. . .

Mr. Hollister and Coach Landry were prefecting at the West End stairs when the crowd started down to the lunchroom. Seeing Anton approach, Mr. Hollister said, intending to be heard, "I'm concerned about that Anton fellow. He's a fine young man, I think." And Coach Landry, not intending to be heard, but heard nonetheless, said to him, "Just keep it in your pants, Hollister."

. . .

Anton drifted with the crowd downstairs to the lunchroom, and then slowly, almost aimlessly, walked on past it and, once out of sight, moved quickly down the corridor to the gym-nasium area and the boiler room. Nobody ever came here except to get to the gym.

Anton ate his lunch in a stall in the men's room, or rather, he ate the apple, having thrown away the sandwich and the cake as soon as he left home this morning. He was safe here. The walls and the cement floor were painted dark green and the massive stalls were made of oak and coated with many layers of varnish. There were no windows and only a single small bulb lit the room. It smelled like church. There was a new men's room on the far side of the gym, with white walls and tan metal booths and lots of light. The boys used that place all the time, but nobody ever came here. Anton sat on the high toilet in the abandoned men's room and ate his apple.

So, it was almost over. And he had made it this far. Only two more classes. Tomorrow he would spend all day drawing. And Sunday too, if he wanted. He finished the apple and continued to sit there, his hands folded in his lap, waiting.

. . .

The rest of the afternoon passed slowly. He was called on three times in French class and twice he gave the answer quickly, almost eagerly. The third time, though, he caught himself, and pretended he didn't know the answer.

He had slipped earlier today with Mr. Hollister, coming out from behind his school face to look at him, and he had almost done it again in French. He would have to be more careful. He could see Miss Pratt looking at him the way she looked at the others, encouraging him to risk an answer, right or wrong, enticing him out. He thought of his real face hang-ing downstairs in the green locker. When Miss Pratt called on him again, she would find he was not even there. The bell rang. Only one more class to go.

Miss Kelly was crazier than usual today. She kept sniffing

and mopping at her nose and hugging herself, but at least she did not call on him. She seemed, in fact, to be deliberately avoiding him. The Prioress's Tale, she was saying, raises the most interesting problems of anti-Semitism in Chaucer's Middle Ages. The Jews of course had been driven out of England in 1290. Which means that Chaucer was probably writing about Jews, and about anti-Semitism, from an accepted tradition rather than from any actual experience of his own. Did they see what this implied about the Christian worldview of that time? Somebody raised his hand to contribute. Anton turned and saw that it was Kevin Delaney, who said that he used to live in Bridgeport and he knew some Jewish kids there and they were just like anybody else; they weren't like New York Jews at all. This got Miss Kelly all upset, though she pretended that he had made an interesting contribution, and then she tried to get them to talk about prejudices and stereotypes in their own lives. Everybody had something to say about this, and they all began to talk at the same time. Anton smiled to himself; they'd do anything rather than read Chaucer. Finally the bell rang and Miss Kelly thanked everyone for an interesting and profitable discussion. In three minutes he would be free.

But instead of just piling her books and papers while they waited for the final bell, Miss Kelly signaled him to the front of the room. She turned her back to the class and edged him around so that nobody would hear her. There was that interested silence. "You can talk quietly, class," she said loudly, and when finally there was a whisper or two, she said, "I hope you found that discussion period helpful, Anton. You see, we all have strange notions about other people sometimes, and sometimes all of us feel that we are outsiders. Do you see? I hope you see that."

Anton began to blush. What a fool the woman was. They

were all looking at him, every one of them. He wanted to kill her; she was killing him. But he only stood there, his eyes lowered.

"I had a little talk with Mr. Hollister, you see." She paused for a moment, but Anton said nothing. "Did you have a good talk with Mr. Hollister? Mr. Hollister is a very unusual man. He has the ability to care. He is a feeling person who feels for others. Mr. Hollister . . . ."

She wasn't talking to him. She was just talking.

Anton raised his eyes and stared at her. He was thinking he could say simply, "He doesn't love you. He will never love you," and she would die, right there, in front of the classroom.

Suddenly Miss Kelly stopped talking and looked at him. "What?" she said. "What is it?" Anton said nothing. "Why are you looking at me that way?" she said. "Stop that. You stop that right now."

It seemed hours before the bell finally rang.

. . .

Anton braced his books under his left arm and walked across the footbridge without looking at the water on either side. There would be ice on the stream by now, at least along the edges. And there would be ice at the claybank. He walked with purpose, but not too fast. He didn't want the others to walk with him or to offer him a ride—not that anyone ever had. But he was careful just the same.

After a half mile, Anton turned off High Street onto Putnam Road and he was completely safe at last. He had a two-mile walk down Putnam, past the woods and the old mill and the claybank, and then another half mile and he would be home. His mother would be in the kitchen, watching television and sipping her muscatel; his father would be out in the cabin working on Gorky. He would show her the bruises and cuts and she would console him, and at night he would lock his bedroom door and draw the things he had felt while she cradled him in her arms. And then he would fall asleep and dream of dying.

He broke a branch and used it as a walking stick. He was an old man taking little steps, propped up by a cane that bent beneath his weight. He walked this way up to the twenty-fifth tree. For the next twenty-five he walked like his mother. And for the next, like his father. He hugged himself, sniffing, and said, in Miss Kelly's voice, "I had a little talk with Mr. Hollister today, Anton." And then for a long time he walked like himself, thinking of Mr. Hollister and how he crossed his legs wrong, and of Miss Kelly. Both of them had seen him with his real face. It was getting harder to hide. He wanted to say real things. He wanted to refuse. But mostly he wanted not to be noticed. And now he was getting hair down there, and he would get big like all the others, and he would be like them in every way except inside, where he could be just himself, and terrified.

He thought of that picture of the old woman on a bridge, screaming. It was called *The Scream,* he thought. He saw the blackness of her open mouth, and he shaped his own mouth like hers, and in a moment he heard the long high wail coming and it would not stop. But finally it did stop. He was dizzy then and black spots sparkled behind his eyes, but he had done it and he felt good. And he had passed the old mill without looking at it once. In a minute he would be at the claybank.

He rounded a turn in the road and there it was, a cliff of clay thirty or forty feet high, half of it chewed away by some huge machine, so that you could see the layers and layers of red and brown and gold and blue-gray. You could spend hours staring at it and never succeed in counting all the colors.

He would never paint in color until he could paint this, he thought. He would never risk it. But then what was he thinking, since he knew he would never paint at all.

There were ice patches here and there, and frozen chunks of clay, and some good patches of shale. Anton took off his mittens and quickly, expertly, slashed at the knuckles of each hand with a small slab of stone. The blood came slowly but he was patient and waited before slashing again. He did not want to go too deep.

And then, somewhere inside, he heard himself think, But what if I don't die. "What if?" he said aloud, and at once he saw himself naked, walking down the school corridor. He was big and hard and he had hair down there. Miss Kelly and Mr. Hollister turned away from him in disgust, and the others all laughed at him, but he did not care. He walked through the corridor and out the front door and down the hill to the little footbridge. He looked back at the school, but nobody had followed him, nobody cared anymore. Without a pause, naked in the cold, he dove into the icy water and swam.

No, he could not let it happen that way. The old way was better. Death would happen if he just waited.

He looked down at his hand and saw that the blood had begun to flow nicely. He made a quick slash vertically across the back of it and then he was done.

On the edge of an ice puddle he found the right piece of frozen clay. It was a silver-blue, the color and weight of steel, and it fitted his palm perfectly. He tossed it in his right hand a few times, got the feel of his fingers around it, and then gathered his books for the short walk home.

He thought of the picture he would draw tonight. A naked man, old, emaciated, tied to something—a dog, a horse, something dead—and out of his mouth small birds come flying.

And as he walked, making up his picture, he beat his right

cheek with the frozen piece of clay. He beat it slowly, rhythm-ically, making the cold flesh swell a little, making the bruise settle into the skin. His cheek grew red and redder, veins surfacing slowly and breaking, preparing the flesh for the purple and black that would follow later.

Anton closed the kitchen door and stood there waiting for his mother to notice. But there was no need to wait; she seemed to have expected it.

"No, oh no," she said, crying. "They've beaten you again, my poor Anton, my poor baby." She held out her arms and he came to her. She cradled him in her lap, whispering over and over, "This is a terrible place, a terrible place. But Anton, my baby, Antosha, you've got your Mutti. You'll always have your Mutti. Your Mutti loves you."

He could smell the sweet wine on her breath and feel her strong arms around him and her soft breasts warming, pro-tecting him. He abandoned himself to the luxury of her grief.

III: THE TERRIBLE MIRROR

A NOVELLA

Look in the terrible mirror of the sky
And not in this dead glass. . . .
                    Wallace Stevens

I

Hunter's wife, as far as any of his colleagues knew, began to exist on the day he married her. She had no past that interested them. She had no present, except as his lively, eager, colorless wife. Her name was Rachel, but she was not even Jewish. She was only a function of Hunter and they accepted her as that. Every great man has some odd inexplicable thing about him. Rachel was his.

·   ·   ·

They had just returned from the President's house and a reception honoring Louise Nevelson. Hunter was having his drink before bed.

"Did you have a nice time?" he said.

"The usual," Rachel said. "But it was a privilege to meet Louise Nevelson, I suppose."

"She's a bore. And the wine was awful."

"Was she boring? What did she say?"

"It's not so much what she says as the way she says it. She listens to her own voice. She watches herself performing. Three sets of eyelashes. My God."

"But you like her work."

"Not anymore."

"Yes," Rachel said, "well." She fluffed the sofa pillows. "I'm going up now. Don't forget the lights, Hunter." She bent over and kissed him.

"Thanks for coming," he said. "I know you hate these things."

" 'Night," she said.

She went upstairs to get ready for bed. She hung up the black mink coat Hunter had given her for Christmas. She put away the diamond and sapphire bracelet, the sapphire ring, the matching earrings—all gifts from Hunter. She undressed and put on her pink flannel nightgown—her comfort gown—the one she wore only after these hideous parties. Hunter had given it to her twenty years before on their first anniversary. She kept it for these special times.

She took from her purse the tiny silver coffee spoon she had stolen from the President's house. It was an ugly spoon, with tarnished filigree on the handle and the bowl. She pulled open the bottom drawer of her dresser and dropped the spoon in with the others. She stared at them blankly for a moment and then she closed the drawer with her foot.

She got into bed and lay in the dark, her eyes open.

Rachel had met Hunter at college when she was a student in his Art History class. Although she was not particularly pretty, Hunter noticed her at once because she was bright and eager and because she listened as if she were passing judgment and the judgment was favorable. After that he noticed she had shining black hair and slanted eyes of a most remarkable green. She noticed that he noticed. She was ten years younger than he.

Hunter was an assistant professor in his first year of teaching, but already he was spoken of as one of the most promising academic sculptors of his generation. Eminent art critics said so. The University had hired him with the promise—against all custom—of tenure within a year. *Esquire* had named him one of the country's Hundred Major Movers Under Thirty. He was it. He was the real thing. Rachel took every course he offered, and in her senior year he chose her as his Teaching Assistant. Still, no one was more surprised than Rachel when, a week after graduation, Hunter asked her to marry him.

They married. Hunter had a Boston show that elicited so much critical enthusiasm that both *Artforum* and *The Arts* did cover stories on him. He was voted tenure and continued his rise to success.

When Rachel got pregnant, she stopped studying medieval art and began studying comparative religion. Religion came in handy, because she was sick during the entire nine months of pregnancy. Doctors could not determine why. Most likely a psychological problem, they said. But when labor began, it went on and on, for two days and into a third. The baby, a boy, was dead at birth. Rachel began to hemorrhage, there were multiple infections, she was dying. But then she didn't die. She had a hysterectomy, followed by a long stay in the hospital. Finally she went home. Hunter would not speak about the baby and Rachel could not. She began studying

Egyptian burial customs, and a little while later Hunter entered his Egyptian period. Everything returned to normal.

Over the years she had moved on from Egyptology to the study of African primitivism, East Indian fetishes, voodoo, zombiism. She began to steal small items at dinner parties. She studied sociology, psychology, Aristotle, Aquinas, the Bible. She memorized the book of Jonah. She stole a tiny figurine, a napkin, a spoon. She began to concentrate on spoons, the uglier the better. Years passed, and she studied, and her silver collection grew. At present, she was reading the Old Testament again, trying to decide which of the sacred books she would memorize next.

They had been married for twenty-one years. Hunter had achieved his promised success, both academic and artistic. Rachel had watched it happen. She was his wife, still carefully slim, still dutifully approving. He gave her everything. They were a perfect, loving couple.

.   .   .

Everybody at the dinner was in literature or the plastic arts except for the President of the University, who had been included as background for Hunter. The President had made a fool of himself by pontificating on subjectivity in art, about which he knew nothing, and to make up for his gaffe they were all talking furiously about life and love.

"We always fall in love with the wrong people," someone said. "Only if we're lucky," someone else said. "What is this preoccupation with love," the host said. "The whole concept is passé. Love is the final deception. Don't you think? No? Blackie agrees with me, don't you, Blackie." "No, you're wrong," Blackie said. "*Life* is the final deception. Love is a daily one." They laughed. Rachel laughed with them and put the dessert fork into her evening bag.

Afterward, standing in a corner of the living room, smiling, brandy in hand, she was approached by Blackie.

"Well," he said, "they tell me that *you* are Hunter's wife." Blackie looked at her conspiratorially. She continued smiling. "He's an absolutely heavenly man. I mean, to look at."

"Yes," she said.

"I'm Blackie," he said, and added, "Prescott. They call me Blackie because of my soul. I've been buying Hunter for years."

Rachel smiled, leaning forward to hear more.

"And what do you do?"

"I'm Hunter's wife."

"That's all?" He gave her that conspiratorial look again. He lowered his voice. "I saw you, you know."

She continued to smile.

"I saw you take the fork. I saw you put it in your purse." Her look never changed.

"Well, you're interesting after all," he said lightly. "Crafty old Hunter. Who'd have guessed it. My dear, we must have lunch. Do you do lunch? Is it your favorite thing in the whole world? No? Do you detest it—I mean absolutely?"

Rachel said nothing.

"Oh good, then we'll do lunch. Tomorrow. The London Tea House? It's divinely camp, with all those toy sandwiches. Say, at twelve? I can't wait to see what you *purloin.* Now I'm going to rescue that handsome husband of yours from Grendel's Mother. Who *is* that bulky woman he's with?"—Hunter was talking with the President's wife—"And *what* is that dress she's wearing? Balenciaga? It's so—how does one say it nicely?—it's so *stuffed,* isn't it. Tomorrow then."

An hour later as they were driving home, Hunter said, "God, I've got to lecture tomorrow," and at once his mind went to the Bloomsburys and Roger Fry and the Omega workshops. "Did you have an awful time?"

"Those people are ridiculous. They're beneath contempt," Rachel said. " 'Life is the final deception. Love is a daily one.'

Honestly. Did anyone there have the slightest idea what life means? Or love?"

Hunter hesitated for a minute, placing her words in the context of his lecture, and then he said, still composing, "Yes, they leave a lot of room for contempt, don't they."

Rachel heaped her contempt upon them all—the drunken President, his vulgar wife, artists and art collectors and teachers of art. She complained as she had wanted to complain for all those years. She exhausted herself raging. Hunter nodded and clucked and listened, but, absorbed as he was in preparing his lecture, he paid attention to only as much as he could use.

The ride home was satisfying to both of them.

· · ·

At lunch the next day Blackie was subdued. "Now you must tell me all about yourself. Every last thing." In a few sentences Rachel told him about her childhood, her education, her marriage to Hunter. "That's it?" Blackie said. "That's your whole life? That's every last thing?"

"That's it," Rachel said.

"Well, my dear, no wonder you steal."

"Spoons."

"Well, that's *some*thing at least. Are you a klepto or is it just a hobby?"

Rachel thought for a while.

"Does your husband know? Does he care? I must say he looks absolutely divine for a man of fifty."

Rachel was still thinking. "It's a coldly rational act," she said. "I like your idea of calling it a hobby. It is, in a way. Except I think of it as revenge."

"Against Hunter," Blackie said.

"No. Against them."

"You're in love! Do you know something?" Blackie said.

"I have never been in love. Not once. I don't know what it feels like even. I have never felt that flutter of the heart. God knows, I've felt flutters everywhere else. My katonks feel like they've been through a Cuisinart. My heart, however, is absolutely intact. Virginal. So stealing seems a small price indeed."

"I don't see the connection."

"Really? You're joking. Between theft and love? But it's so clear."

"I don't see what you're getting at."

"Well, the basic question for you, my dear, is this: what do you *want?*"

．　．　．

Rachel had pulled the dresser drawer out onto the carpet and was examining the contents. A chartreuse napkin, polyester. An aluminum coaster. A tiny porcelain owl with googly eyes and a big smile. And spoons, plain and filigreed, bent, bitten, permanently stained. Forks. A butter knife. Everything was ugly, hideous. She had been very discriminating in her choice of things.

The first time had been nearly ten years earlier. She was sitting at a dinner table as the talk went on around her, through her, as if she did not exist, and she sat there smiling and nodding, showing herself involved. She was thinking of what she might do if she were someone else: leap up from the table, fling her wineglass at the wall, yank the tablecloth and send everything on it crashing to the floor. But then she felt her reason give way. She seemed to have left her body and to be watching the scene from above.

In her mind, she saw herself turn to face the man beside her. She watched from above as her other self, seated calmly at the table, took her coffee spoon and inserted it carefully beneath the man's eyelid, pushed it in, turned it, and scooped out his eye.

At once she came back to herself and, still smiling, dropped the spoon into her evening bag, casually, as if it were a key or a lipstick or an earring that pinched. She paid no attention to what she was doing and neither did anyone else.

That was ten years ago. By now she had so far tamed the irrational that from the moment she was seated at table, she knew which item she would steal. The only question was when. And this was what her life came down to.

Could this be what she wanted?

. . .

"I saw that Blackie creep today," Hunter said. "He wants to do a retrospective of my stuff in New York."

"At a gallery?"

"He owns the Prescott."

"Oh yes, he said that."

"He said you had lunch with him."

"Yes."

"Yes? Just like that? Yes?"

"Yes. We had lunch. At the London Tea House."

"Do you usually have lunch with people? Do you go out all the time and I don't even know it?"

"No. Why are you so cross?"

"Why did you go? With *him,* of all people."

"He asked me to."

"You didn't tell me that."

"I had a cream cheese and walnut sandwich. He had . . ."

"God! Well, what did you talk about? Did you talk about something? Was there a subject? A topic?"

"We talked about love and theft."

Hunter looked at her as if she were crazy.

She looked at him as if he were a stranger.

. . .

After this, Rachel did not steal for a while. She begged off going to parties on the grounds that she was not herself.

Hostesses tried to meet this excuse without a smile—indeed when had she ever been herself? and what on earth was that likely to be?—and when Hunter absolutely had to go, he went alone. Without Rachel at his side, smiling and nodding and asking the necessary questions, he found the routine exhausting and more than once he asked when she thought she might start accompanying him again. "Possibly never," she said, and Hunter stared at her, amazed at this new and difficult woman. It was the Change, he supposed.

She gave up her study of the Bible. She had memorized Chapter 22 of Genesis, Abraham's sacrifice of Isaac, before she realized that what fascinated her about it was God's terrible inhumanity. She'd seen enough inhumanity in her life. She put the Bible aside for good.

She began reading about moral issues and progressed rapidly, if sketchily, from Barth and Niebuhr to Bok's *Secrets* and Rich's *On Lies, Secrets, and Silence,* and from Rich to a lot of other books on feminism, a special kind of morality. In a matter of months she discovered she was not really interested in morality or in feminism, she was interested in herself. She found she was unlike moralists of any kind; she felt no anger against God or society or men or sexual roles or even Hunter, poor Hunter. But she was angry nonetheless.

She decided, finally, that she must be angry at herself. Who was she, after all? What was she? She had used up more than half a perfectly good life and she had not lived one day of it. Hunter was a mess and he lived his life sloppily, but at least he created things. She had created nothing, good or bad. She *was* nothing.

From her long-forgotten Catholic past she called up the notion of the one unforgivable sin: the sin against the Holy Ghost. This must be it, she thought, this refusal to live one's own life. She had committed the unforgivable sin and hadn't even noticed.

She could make this moment a turning point; she knew that. And so she did.

She resolved to start attending those hideous parties once again. She would appear to be the dutiful anonymous wife of the sculptor. She would live her life with a vengeance.

.   .   .

She would begin living life with a vengeance soon, but right now she was doing work for Hunter in the big new studio behind the house. They had built the studio a year ago. It had a guest room upstairs, and in the studio itself there was plenty of good light, ample work space for Hunter and an assistant, and all kinds of shelving to store Hunter's stuff—his young work, old casts, things he liked too much to sell, sculptures partly roughed out and then abandoned, work in progress, plans for new work. It was all there, in some semblance of chronological order, but it had never been properly catalogued and Rachel had agreed to give the job a try.

A complete catalogue was the first step toward Hunter's New York show. He had finally agreed to Blackie's idea of a retrospective because there was no way he could turn it down. It would be the seal of success on his reputation. It would place him, definitively, among contemporary artists. It would make him rich and famous. Or so Blackie kept saying. My *dear*.

Rachel was poking about among the Egyptian stuff, trying to get some idea of the time and effort a catalogue would entail. Hunter had told her to begin with his medieval things and go on to whatever came next—the gods and goddesses, he thought—and then the Egyptian and the African primitive stuff. He was right about the chronology, of course, despite his uncertainty. Rachel had no uncertainty at all. She remembered each piece as if she had done it herself. Hunter was already at the end of his affair with medieval art at the time they married and she remembered vividly how he had floundered around, having worked through the Middle Ages and not knowing what to do next. That was when he discovered the gods and goddesses. Rachel was pregnant at the time, studying comparative religion, and she could still recall Hunter's funny earnestness as he explained how medieval concentration on the figures of Jesus and Mary had led him naturally to the great cultic figures of other religions; he had interrupted himself to write down "great cultic figures of other religions" and she had seen those same words a year later in the catalogue produced for his Divinities show.

Rachel smiled to herself. Hunter was a miser of the spirit. He wasted nothing. Everything—feeling, thought, desire— everything cycled back into his art.

She fingered the smooth lion head of the goddess Sekhmet, the earliest of Hunter's Egyptian pieces. Next to it was Horus, the falcon-headed sun god. And then Anubis, the dog, lord of the necropolis. Hunter had done Anubis more than a year after she lost the baby. He went silent. She had a hysterectomy. That was when they began slipping away from each other.

The statue of Anubis was unlike any of his other work. It was not derived from or inspired by something else; it was simply a copy—without distortion, without interpretation— of the statue found in Tutankhamen's tomb. It was of black wood, with gold leaf on the ears and around the eyes, and the eyes themselves were of obsidian. The proud head was held up and seemed to pull away; the thin line of the mouth was tight in refusal. Perhaps because it was only a copy, Hunter had never shown it. Rachel stood before the statue, motionless.

In her mind, she saw herself turn and walk to Hunter's worktable. She watched from above as her other self selected a long pointed chisel and a leaded mallet and, with awful ease, destroyed the god's face. Her heart stopped beating. But at once she came back to herself and simply reached out and, with the nail of her index finger, gouged away a tiny piece of wood from the left side of the dog's mouth. A white space appeared there suddenly; Anubis, keeper of the necropolis, looked almost as if he were smiling.

That night at a dinner for Josef Albers, Rachel was her old self, eager and lively and colorless. Her dinner companions were bored. But she smiled and smiled, and Hunter was reassured, though even to him it seemed a very long dinner.

As they finished coffee and got up to leave, Rachel slipped the ugly spoon out of her purse and placed it on the table. The action was open, casual. She paid no attention to what she was doing and neither did anyone else.

．　．　．

Hunter was blocked for the moment, a good time for this to happen since all his energies should be going into his show. But being blocked left him restless, angry. He wasn't really human unless he had some work under way, or at least in the thinking stage. It was maddening. His powers of conception and execution, his sheer mastery of craft, were all at their peak. This was the time to take on a masterwork, one that would summon his mature talent and skills.

At times like this he always went to Rachel. He had found that just talking through his problem very often resolved it. He went to her now. She listened, as always, and she sympathized. But for once it did not take. She was busy cataloguing his work and the rest of the time she seemed caught up in herself. He had never seen her so preoccupied. He didn't like it. He preferred the old dreamy days when she sat around memorizing things. The last time she'd done that was when she tackled Abraham and Isaac. Since then she'd become stranger by the day.

. . .

"How is the catalogue going? Have you begun the actual work or are you still doing the overview?"

"I've begun, in a way."

"What do you think?"

"It's like looking at your work from above, Hunter. Sort of a god's-eye view on where your mind was at any given moment. Where your heart was."

Hunter stopped eating and looked at her.

"Where your soul was," she said.

"And?"

"It's interesting. It all points to something, but right now I don't know what."

Hunter was silent for a while, and then he said, "After this show, I want to get you something very special. Jewelry? A diamond necklace? With emeralds? Something that costs."

"A face-lift? Breast augmentation?"

Hunter laughed.

"A personality transplant?"

"What's the matter, Rachel? What's this really about?"

"Sorry. It must be—capital C—the Change."

A short silence. He wanted to shift his mind to her, to what she was saying, but it was simply too great an effort. She sat there looking the same as always: black hair, green eyes, slim as when they first married; she was more or less the perfect wife. Still, he owed it to her to give her some real hard thought, soon. He couldn't be happy unless she was happy.

"Blackie says he'd like to come here," Hunter said, "and take a long look at everything. Every last *thing*. I told him you had only begun the catalogue and he ought to wait, but he was adamant. He said he just wanted to have a *look*. He made it sound dirty."

"Of course he did. My *dear*."

A long silence.

"I'll tell him to wait," Hunter said.

A long strained silence.

"At least we've got nothing for the rest of this month," Hunter said. "No parties, no dinners, no receptions of any kind. We're free."

"Really? I've begun to look forward to them, in a way."

.　　.　　.

Rachel was counting: Hunter had done eight—no, nine—metal sculptures of the ibis. The ibis alone, his long curved bill plunged beneath the water. The ibis alone, neck extended, head cocked, listening. The ibis alone, ready for flight. Variations on these. Two ibises looking past each other. Two ibises leaning together in fear. Three ibises in a cluster. And then, as if Hunter had at last discovered where these birds were taking him, there was the final, complicated frightening work: on a tiny pedestal eight birds huddled together, eight blind heads thrust upward toward the sun, sixteen impossibly long legs bent backward in the middle. The soldering of the legs had gone blue and black and gray; the metal dull and beaded. The whole thing spoke fragility and fear and a terrible finitude.

Rachel ran her finger down one of the long legs, bent backward in the middle, preposterously thin. She caressed the knob where soldering joined the upper and lower part of the leg, making a kind of reversed kneecap. Gently at first, as if she were testing for sturdiness, she wrapped her hand around the leg, pressing her thumb just above the joint, while below the joint, from the other side of the leg, she pulled toward her, gently, with her index finger. The leg was sturdy indeed. She pressed hard with her thumb, pulled hard with all four fingers. She pulled harder until the whole sculpture shook, the bodies trembling on the long thin legs, metal clanging against metal, but still the soldering held. It took her a long time and considerable effort before the joint gave way and the leg snapped.

That night there was a dinner for Arts Development. Rachel smiled and her green eyes glittered as she played the devoted anonymous wife. At the end of dinner, she opened her purse and took out an ugly silver spoon and placed it on the table. Her work was progressing well.

. . .

Blackie gave up trying to convince Hunter to let him examine every last thing in his studio and concentrated his energies on Rachel. He was dying of curiosity, he told her. He was desperate to have a look. He *needed* to have a look; how else could he plan a retrospective? At least they should talk. At lunch? This Friday? He had a Trustees dinner at the Fogg on Friday evening and he was flying in from New York for that, so if they had lunch earlier in the day, it would be heavenly. He could kill two birds with one trip, so to speak. Rachel had come in from Hunter's studio where she'd just finished her work on the two ibises looking past each other and so she could not help smiling at the nice congruency of Blackie's killing two birds. She agreed to lunch.

"I adore Boston," Blackie was saying over his veal Oscar. "It's such a provincial town, really, and it's preserved its provinciality intact, don't you think? The tacky little restaurants, I mean, and the Hill, and the North End, and the absolutely *dedicated* scruffiness of the Combat Zone. I sometimes think I should move back. Do you think I could endure it?"

He was trying very hard, but Rachel was not herself: not eager or lively; not the least interested in drawing him out. She seemed almost surly. Where was the closet kleptomaniac he knew and admired? Where had she gone?

"Yoo-hoo," he said, "I'm over here." He reached across the table and ticked a fingernail against her large diamond ring.

"What is it you want?" she said.

"Bonka, bonk," he said. "We're all business today, aren't we. Well, I want to represent Hunter in New York. I want to mount a retrospective of his work. And, as I've been telling him every day now for absolute ages, I want to have a good look at *every*thing he's done, right from the beginning."

"Why can't you wait? The catalogue's not even half done."

"I want to *see* the whole run of his work. I want a comprehensive overview."

"You're afraid he'll suppress some important piece?"

"My *dear*."

"Or is it me? Are you afraid I'll omit something? Or suppress something? Or destroy it?"

Blackie looked at her.

"Through carelessness, of course. Or is it malice you suspect?"

"My dear, you're absolutely fascinating."

"What is it you really want? Him?"

Blackie stared at her for a minute, picked up his fork, and then put it down again. "I hadn't really thought about it, but I suppose you're right. I do want him. I joke so much about sex that it never occurred to me it might be true. How . . . intuitive you are." His voice went higher, louder, the old Blackie. "But not to worry, my dear; it's only lust."

"No, it's something else. You want to possess him without his knowing it. You tell yourself it's his body you want, his thing . . . all right, his cock . . . but it isn't that at all. You want to penetrate the mystery in him. You want to lie down with his soul."

"My *dear;* you're *too* shocking."

"But that's his." She leaned toward him with a terrible concentration and her voice was low and final. "It's mine."

Blackie turned away, flushed, and then he took a long drink of water and choked on it.

Rachel was silent.

"My dear," he finally said. "What a thing to say. And what *intensity*. You ought to be some kind of artist yourself, you know. I mean, just think of it. You've got everything it takes. You've got love and theft and a good brain, I suppose—not that a brain matters—and now I see you've got this marvelous intensity. Why, you're *exactly* like Hunter."

They talked pleasantly after that, more or less, but they did not part friends.

That night, at the Fogg dinner, Rachel and Blackie were seated opposite each other. After coffee and brandy, as they were about to rise, Rachel took the dessert fork from her purse and, though she knew Blackie was watching her, she placed it on the table.

Afterward, as they were getting their coats, Blackie leaned into her and said, "Exactly like him, my dear. Exactly."

.   .   .

A week had passed since her last encounter with Blackie and during that week Rachel frequently paused at whatever she was doing and wondered what he meant: "You're exactly like Hunter." And once, as she forged ahead in the catalogue of Hunter's work—moving from his gods and goddesses to his Egyptians and Africans and East Indians, and on and on— once, just for a moment, she thought she understood. There was a stunning correlation between the subject matter of Hunter's sculpture and her own flighty studies. But how could Blackie know that? And how did that make them alike? Besides, Hunter's sculptures were works of art while her studies had been acts of desperation. She shrugged and went on with the job of cataloguing Hunter's life.

Now it was Friday and she had finished her work for the day. She closed her notebook, getting ready to leave, but on her way out of the studio she paused a moment before the

African pieces. There was one she liked particularly: a crouching black warrior carved from ebony, gorgeous in his nakedness, with only a necklace and a spear to hide him. She touched the point of his spear, caressed his head and shoulders, and then methodically, as if she were a physician performing a necessary operation, she took a penknife and sliced a thin sliver of wood from his heel. She dropped the penknife into her pocket.

At the door of the studio she turned back. For some time now Hunter had been at work on a sculpture he was keeping secret. It was Abraham's sacrifice of Isaac, she knew, because he left marked books all around the house and because he had the four Rembrandt prints newly framed for display above his desk and because he mentioned Abraham or Isaac or both at least ten times a day. Nonetheless he thought of it as secret. His masterwork, he called it once, and blushed at his own vanity. He had said nothing more about the sculpture itself, only that it was to be in stone and it would take him at least a year. He had begun, as always, with a clay model.

She approached his worktable, immaculate, uncluttered. There was no sign of the pipe and wire and wood he had used for armature; his chisels, points, pitching tool, and rasps were all hung in place and ready for use, later, when he would start over again in stone. The clay model itself was covered with a cage of damp cloth. She paused in front of it, a small thing, no more than a foot high, mounted on a turntable. She had never looked at his work in progress; she had never asked to look. It was a violation of privacy, of intimacy. She could not bring herself to look now. And then she did.

She lifted the cloth carefully with both hands and laid it to one side, revealing the finished clay model of Hunter's Abraham and Isaac. The body of the young boy was stretched across the stone altar. An old man—his father—arched above him, his ancient face turned away in horror, as he held the long knife poised, ready to strike. It was a scene of terrible barbarism, of superhuman cruelty. Hunter had caught the old man's obedience and the willing victim's sacrifice.

Rachel examined the work with a professional eye. It was good. It was very very good. It was exciting. God's inhumanity to man.

After a while her professional eye failed her. She found herself looking at the work uncritically, feeling her way inside, surrendering to it. She became the obedient murderer, the victim sanctified. And then, without any warning and for only a single instant, she became Hunter. At once she understood what Blackie meant.

She moved out that afternoon. She left no note, no explanation, only a drawer full of ugly stolen silver.

And Hunter, seeing she was gone, said "Why?" And "Why?"

2

After his wife left him, Hunter reacted in the usual ways. At first he avoided seeing people because he was ashamed and guilty, then he got angry and smashed things around a lot, and finally he just gave up and took to drink like everybody else.

What surprised Hunter most was that he had nobody to turn to, that for all these years Rachel had been his only friend. Feeling betrayed and despondent, he drank. Then Blackie reappeared in his life and insisted Hunter either mount his show at once or forfeit the gallery space and time to some other artist. Hunter ambled through his studio looking at the work Rachel had only half-finished cataloguing, noting the signature marks of revenge she had left on each, and because this discovery showed him how hurting and desperate she must have been, he wept for a long time and he drank. He wrote Blackie, telling him a show was no longer possible. He drank to forget and he drank to punish himself and he drank because he was guilty. He went to bed drunk and in the morning he awoke, huddled in his big empty bed, alone, wanting only to be drunk all over again.

In his second year of drinking Hunter discovered sex. It became a way of escaping the memory of Rachel and a way of punishing her too. He had been faithful to her for all those years of marriage. Despite lots of opportunities, he had not strayed once, not even with Reba Cairn, that red-haired painter of indeterminate age who told everybody at the Registration Day party that she simply had to have Hunter before the night was over. She was going to suck his cock, she said, even if she had to scramble around under the table to do it. Though she failed that night, Reba continued her assaults on him throughout the next three months. She phoned him at the office and at the studio and at home, she attacked him physically in private and in public, and one memorable snowy night in December she stood beneath his window yelling for him to come down and get sucked off like a man. Then suddenly at Christmas she left the University, having married a rich graduate student from Iman, and was not heard from again. And all that time he had remained faithful to Rachel.

Hunter's late discovery of sex came about because of his drinking. He had gone to a dinner party at the Pattersons', who always seemed to have trouble getting the food to the table. That night they were particularly slow about it, so that by dinnertime Hunter had downed several straight whiskeys, and by the time they served dessert he was thoroughly smashed. They gave him lots of coffee after that and by 1

A.M., when all the guests had gone, he was still smashed but he looked pretty good, and so Mrs. Patterson drove him home. Perhaps because of the challenge his famed fidelity presented or perhaps because he just looked so needy, Mrs. Patterson put him to bed and joined him there. He rose to the occasion at once and then again later, with twists and variations of Mrs. Patterson's special invention, and by morning he had discovered sex as a more colorful escape than the stimulation and stupor provided by alcohol.

He did not for a minute confuse this brand of sex with either passion or lust. When they were first married, he had felt passion for Rachel, and sometimes lust, but after the loss of their child, passion was something he reserved for sculpting and his only lust was for perfection.

This new kind of sex was a purely physical activity, providing new ways for the body to activate and then numb the senses. It was the ancient ritual he had read about, but with the difference offered by a constant change of partners—indeed a blurring of partners was the best—so that names and faces ceased to matter; only body parts mattered, and whatever pleasure could be wrung from them. Keeping it up, keeping it hard, forcing the other body to respond to the prolongation of a kind of gasping kiss, the subtleties of a sudden thrust, the wet exhausting push of one body into another so that flesh churned beneath other flesh, until both of them came, together, and they said yes, and yes, and this is what life is all about, this is *all* that life is all about, eternal present, fucking, sucking your heart and soul into mine, though they knew—Hunter knew—that hearts and souls had almost nothing to do with it. And then, of course, the aftermath, the discovery that they had always been two separate people, that his own skin was the only skin he would ever inhabit, and that sex—for him—was a vain attempt to end his endless isolation.

Still, sex at least was something real and for a while Hunter pursued it recklessly. He was fifty-one, with a gray beard and a little roll of flesh around his waist, and yet he had no trouble attracting women; he moved with ease and desperation among a variety of faculty wives and Teaching Assistants and women he met in dating bars. He was a man on his way around the bend and they found that interesting, and besides he was an artist. He drank and fucked them all and drank some more.

Sometime in his second year of drinking, the sex year, Hunter's self-destruction had consequences he had not foreseen. Blackie was in town on business and decided to give himself the treat of a quick look at Hunter and was appalled at what he saw. "This can't go on, you know," Blackie said, "you're going to destroy yourself." Hunter was slumped on the couch and, out of annoyance, just for the hell of it, he put down his glass and stretched full length and said to Blackie, "I could destroy *you,* and you'd love it," and he took Blackie to bed. The sex was fine, but doing it just for spite was sort of sick, Hunter thought, but who cared really: it was just another body with other body parts. He forgot the whole affair by the next afternoon.

Blackie, however, did not forget. He kept phoning and leaving messages, showing up on weekends with little gifts, talking all the while about the physical union of their two spirits. *Spirits,* no less. Hunter could not deal with nonsense of that dimension and felt justified in driving Blackie away by whatever means were required. Mockery didn't work nor did sarcasm, but silent contempt was very effective and Blackie finally quit. What stayed with Hunter was not the memory of their souls' union but his own cruelty to a man who had wished him only good. He handled this the way he handled everything; he had a drink and found some woman to screw and in time he forgot everything, nearly.

. . .

What snapped him out of this was, of course, absurd. He awoke one morning in spring and heard the birds in the trees and realized suddenly that it would be easier to do something about his life than to go on like this. He got up and looked in the mirror at the wreckage he had created and then he showered, scrubbing away despair like so much dirt. It was that easy for him, so easy it was frightening. For a moment he felt as if in some miraculous way he had been delivered into the hands of a loving and comfortable god.

He headed at once for his studio where he removed the stiff cloths from the clay model of his Abraham and Isaac. He stepped back to assess it coldly and found that he could not catch his breath. It had hairline cracks from its long neglect, but it was nonetheless an astonishing piece of work. The wildness and the barbarity, the superhuman cruelty, the eagerness of the victim: how had he done it? It was overpowering even in this small scale. Could he summon the courage to attempt it life-size? His hands began to tremble and he felt the stale booze rise in his throat. He covered the model at once and left the studio.

Within a month, however, he was cutting the rough form of his Abraham and Isaac out of an enormous block of white Vermont marble. In no time he saw it was a disaster. He started over, this time with soapstone because it handled so much easier. And then again. And again. So it went for the better part of a year, until he was forced to conclude that his talent had run out. He was just another fake sculptor who knew what to do and how to do it, but lacked the talent to do it himself.

Vision alone was not enough. He could see the form inside the stone, but he couldn't get it out. He lacked the right control, and he cut away too little and then too much. He had never found the artist's balance between making it happen and letting it happen. He knew, always too late, what had gone wrong.

He was cursed with knowing what to do and how to do it. He had craft, not talent. But he could teach craft. He would give up drink and women and all the rest of it and put his considerable energies into teaching. Save a life. Be a teacher. The life you save may be et cetera.

3

Hunter had been teaching with great success for no more than a year when the idea of a protégé began to form in his mind. Someone he could fashion in his own image and likeness. Someone he could teach the secrets of craft. And, most important, someone who could forge his way beyond craft to that austere country inhabited by genius. He discovered Paul Bates.

Paul Bates was thin to the point of emaciation. He had long black hair and a beard. His arms and even his hands were thick with that same black hair. He always looked lost.

Hunter disliked Paul at sight, but by the end of the first semester Paul's talent had won him over. Hunter began to work more closely with him. He offered him the kind of criticism he reserved for the truly talented. Paul listened to what he said and did it. His attack changed. The craft he learned from Hunter allowed him to put aside the work that came to him so easily and to tap deeper resources; he began to produce less finished but more challenging work. It showed complexity. It showed ambition. It was stronger and richer than anything he had done before. Paul Bates was beginning.

When Paul finished his degree, Hunter hired him as a studio assistant. The pay was minimal—no one could possibly live on it—but Paul was as oblivious to the money as he was to everything else. He said the pay was just fine; all he cared about was having some time and a place to work and, of course, the chance to study under a master. "Don't be sarcastic," Hunter said, just in case.

Each afternoon Paul would stand beside Hunter as they looked at Paul's work in progress. Hunter would gaze and nod and gaze some more. Sometimes he would say, "yes," or "uh-huh," or "that's good." And sometimes he would remind him of basic physical facts: "the female skull is always slightly smaller than the male" or "a man's muscles make up about half his total weight." But mostly he said nothing until Paul had decided the sculpture was finished or that he had taken it as far as he could. Then Hunter became all action. He circled the little platform, commenting, praising, his hands in constant motion, his attention fixed completely on the work, deliberately unaware of Paul's emotional response. "Just listen to me now, and try to concentrate on what I'm saying. You'll have time to cry or celebrate later." And he would trace an invisible line with his fingertip. "This is good," Hunter would say. "This is very nicely done." But then he would trace another invisible line and say, "But look at this, right here. It's not a line, it's a blank spot. It's empty. You lose definition. You're rushing. You're going too fast. We're talking basic technique here. Craft always comes back to basics and basics require patience and time and meticulous, loving care. You've got to love the chisel, and the feel and the smell of stone, and the pressure in your hand and wrist as you bear down . . . well, you know all that. But *do* it."

It was at this period in his development that the scandal occurred. Paul was discovered sleeping in his studio classroom with a graduate student. She was only one in a series, for Paul, emaciated or not, was pursued by women. The incident would have been successfully hushed up except for one sensational detail: the classroom was where Paul actually lived. Nobody cared whom he slept with, but everyone from the custodian to the provost cared very much that—in open violation of health, fire, and decency laws—he had taken up residence in a classroom. It turned out he showered at the gym. He ate at McDonald's. He kept his clothes in a locker at the bus station. All the facts of his private life were suddenly public.

When Hunter heard about it, he took a deep breath and made a quick decision. "This is ridiculous," he said to Paul. "Come live in my studio." And Paul did.

A year passed, and under Hunter's constant tutelage, Paul came into a certain mastery of craft. Hunter's criticism became more emphatic and more demanding. "No. No. No. Obscurity is not profundity, Paul. Confusion is not mystery. Look *here!*" He rapped the wood urgently with his knuckles. "You can go on and make a career out of stuff like this, you can probably even get rich doing it, but you'll know and I'll know that it's easy and cheap. It's fakery, in a way. And if you're going to take rich gifts like yours and use them for this kind of stuff, I want nothing to do with it." And then he'd soften and say, "And I know you want nothing to do with it either. You want to do the best. You *must* do the best. So stop leaving shadows that are supposed to make us think *you*'re deep. The truth is *you*'re irrelevant. It's the work that matters. Okay? Okay. Good God, you're all red in the face. I'm not attacking you, Paul, I'm attacking the work. And it's good. It's very very good. It just has problems. Now, why don't we have a drink and we'll just talk about it."

Still later, when Paul had achieved his own sure touch, Hunter became ruthless. "Oh for God's sake, Paul, why don't you just use an axe. Look at this thing. It's not an arm, it's a lump. It's some kind of hideous excrescence. And look at *this.* Don't you see the shape the stone wants to take. Your material has to be listened to. Sculpting is invention in every sense of the word: you make something out of the material but only when you've discovered what's there. You *find* it. Right? Well, you know that." He found in each piece of sculpture the hidden lines and form and substance that Paul had failed to set free. It was splendid, really, Hunter said. It just wasn't finished.

Things went on like this until Hunter at last desisted. The work was as near finished as work can get. It was good. Period.

Though Hunter did not really like the idea, he agreed that perhaps Paul Bates was ready for his first show.

. . .

On the night of Paul's opening, Hunter was blinded and disfigured in a freak car accident. The show was at the Kaska Gallery on Newbury Street and Hunter had gone early to have a drink with the owner and to bolster Paul's courage and to convince himself that he had been right in letting Paul exhibit. He had seen the sculptures over and over in the studio, but a gallery always offered them in a new light, and Hunter wanted to see what new things would emerge. He walked slowly among all the perfectly lit, perfectly mounted pieces, and saw them suddenly as misconceived, unfinished, pretentious. How could he have been so mistaken? There was no doubt in his mind that he had lost the small talent he had once possessed, but had he lost his critical sense as well? He felt the panic mounting in him as he realized that Paul would never be a better sculptor than he was right now, and right now he was second rate. In that instant of realization his love for Paul, his hope for him, turned to disillusion, then to disgust. Hunter left the gallery, half blind with rage. But he had made his decision: he would give up teaching and Paul Bates would have to leave at once.

A block from home his car was struck broadside by a small van running a light. The driver slammed on his brakes just in time, so the collision merely dented the door and shattered the side window of Hunter's car. But at the moment of impact, Hunter cast a horrified look at the oncoming van and caught the thousands of tiny glass particles across the eyes and nose and mouth. It was merely the freakiness of the accident that left him blind and disfigured.

.   .   .

After the accident, Paul took care of everything. He engaged doctors, ratified their decisions about treatment and surgery, took care of the Blue Cross nightmare. He was Hunter's sole support in the hospital, and when Hunter returned home blotched and patchy looking, Paul was there to support him still. He had already curtailed his time with the succession of girls who visited him nights and now he cut them out completely. He hired a cleaning woman from Thailand who spoke enough English to understand what must be done and who willingly did the extra things they needed, like making lunch for Hunter when Paul had to teach. And he taught himself how to cook.

Paul insisted that Hunter sleep downstairs in the guest room. It was near the kitchen and had its own bathroom and, most important, Paul could keep an eye on it from his own room above the studio. He made Hunter's comfort his first thought in everything. Within weeks, Paul had given up life as a working sculptor and had become a nurse and companion and friend.

He did not like being any of these things. He felt nothing for Hunter except vague resentment for all that criticism, but Hunter, he knew, loved him like a son, and believed in him as an artist, and so taking care of Hunter was a matter of gratitude and Paul did what he had to do.

As for Hunter, he was not concerned about love and belief

and gratitude. He was constantly furious and he had not yet found the courage to tell Paul he must leave.

He was blind. This was the awful, unalterable fact he had to deal with and he was simply not prepared to do so. For the first month, while his face was being repaired and his eyes attended to, he asked how this could have happened to him. Why? And then, as always, why?

On leaving the hospital, he pushed disappointment and self-pity aside and settled comfortably into hatred—of Paul, of himself, of everyone who was not blind. But he hated Paul particularly. He needed Paul.

"What is this mess? What is it?"

"It's your eggs," Paul said, still patient after more than a month of this. "Fried. Over lightly."

"They aren't hot." He poked them with his finger.

"They *were* hot."

"I'm slow getting dressed. I'm blind, you see, Paul. Blind people tend to be slow about such things. It's never been explained why."

"I'll cook you some new eggs."

"Never mind. I'll eat them this way."

Silence for a moment and then a pained yelp from Hunter. He had put his finger in his coffee cup.

"The *coffee* is hot," Paul said.

"Are you laughing at me?" An accusation. "Are you?" Hunter sat back in his chair and touched his reconstructed mouth, gently, with his napkin. "You know, Paul, I think you're actually developing a talent. For ridicule."

This was as close as they had come to talking about Paul's show.

They faced each other across the table now in silence. Hunter waited for a response. After a long moment, Paul asked him if he would like more coffee.

Paul was finding this gratitude business harder and harder.

. . .

Dr. Forrest made his weekly visit and repeated what he had said before. Hunter should regain at least partial vision. Indeed, there was nothing to prevent his seeing right now. Nothing physical. He waited for a response.

Hunter was sitting in the back garden. He had spoken to no one all day and he did not speak now.

The doctor's annoyance turned to anger.

"Are you *pleased* to be this way?" he said. "Does it give you some perverse satisfaction to *refuse* to see?"

Hunter gave him such a look of scorn that for a moment Dr. Forrest wondered if he *did* see. On the chance that he did, Dr. Forrest winked at him so that Hunter would know that he knew. Dr. Forrest had dealt with hysterics before.

. . .

"I've brought you a present," Paul said.

Hunter was still sitting in the back garden where Paul had left him after breakfast that morning. It was six o'clock.

"Hunter?" Paul said. "I've got a present for you. It's inside. Come on in and take a look." He winced. For once Hunter did not pounce on him.

In the living room, Paul said, "Here, next to your chair. Just sit, and then turn to your left as if you were going to pick up a book, and you'll feel it."

"It's glass," Hunter said, "and steel. Or maybe it's glass and aluminum. Or chrome. It seems to be six or seven stacked boxes, units; some kind of stereo?"

"Terrific," Paul said, "exactly." He watched Hunter move his hands expertly along the face of the stereo, exploring buttons, station settings, the glass itself. "Actually," Paul said proudly, "it's a Sony F-V7."

Hunter fingered the ribbon slung diagonally across the stereo. There was a ribbon with a big bow down near the bottom. Hunter had been astonished at the idea of a present from Paul and he had been filled with bitterness at the realization that he would never see it. But it was the ribbon that moved him to tears. That stupid, talented, disappointing lump, with his marvelous articulate hands, had taken the trouble to tie a bow around a present. . . . Hunter cleared his throat.

"This is a heavy-duty stereo," Paul said, talking fast. "Let me tell you. Here we've go eighty watts integrated amp, quartz digital tuner, with eight station presets. How's that! You don't have to fiddle around finding your station; you just decide ahead of time what you want and then later you press here and it tunes in automatically. What else? Okay, you've got front load, direct drive, linear tracking turntable—very nice—automatic reverse cassette, a ten-inch three-way speaker system. And that's it. Well, there's a nine-band graphic equalizer, too. And down here is storage for records and cassettes. I got some basic Mozart, Vivaldi, Telemann stuff. Pachelbel's canon. Nothing adventurous. No heavy metal." He was out of breath, excited.

"I wish I could see it," Hunter said.

"Well, listen, maybe you will." Paul was seated on the footstool, leaning close. "The doctor said it could happen."

Paul had lived here for three years with his terrible music blaring away half the night. He had eaten a thousand meals at Hunter's table. He had had hours and hours of criticism, of time—free and generous—and he had never so much as said thank you. And now he was giving this present. Was this the end?

"Here's the power button," Paul said. "And here's how you control the radio, and here . . . " Hunter listened dutifully, terrified he was about to be abandoned once again.

·   ·   ·

At first Hunter played the stereo only in the late afternoon so that when Paul came in from the studio, he'd find him listening. But after a while Hunter got caught up in the music itself. He passed hours listening to Bach and Mozart and Telemann.

And then Hunter discovered the preachers. He pressed the wrong button by accident, and before he had time to change the setting, a voice boomed out at him, "It's Jesus, Jesus, Jeeee-zus alone who loves you to death." A chorus of voices shouted "Ay-men, Ay-men." For the first time since the accident, Hunter laughed out loud.

After this he tuned in on the preachers first thing after breakfast. He listened for five or ten minutes at a time. Then he would sit in silence and contemplate this unique exhibition of human folly. Hunter was not a religious man. His Biblical sculptures proceeded from a lifelong obsession with Bible stories, not from an interest in theology. All the same, he was amused and outraged by the way these preachers tortured Bible texts into serving their own ends. They always ended up asking for money. Moses in the bullrushes, Sodom and Gomorrah, Absalom's golden hair: no matter what the text, the point was to send money.

One morning he heard the names of Abraham and Isaac, but he had tuned in too late to get the context. He got only the message: "Just like for Abraham, God can turn things around for *you*. Now, we want to double the number of missionary brothers we have planting the seed in Africa today. I *know* there are thousands out there who can send in one thousand dollars right now, *and,* I promise you, we will send you right away this genuine anodized silver medallion saying "I make a difference." *Do* you? Do you make a difference? You *can*. Send that check or money order right now. And take these words from me: *God* . . . can turn things *around* . . . for *you*."

This had stopped being funny. Hunter flicked to another

station and surrendered himself once again to the mathematical precision of Bach.

.   .   .

"Speaking of money," Hunter said.

They were eating dinner and had not been speaking at all. It was one of Hunter's silent days. Paul knew them and did not speak until spoken to. He was careful to appear more laconic than Hunter himself.

"I've got enough," Paul said.

"That's what I've been wondering about. That stereo you bought for me, Paul, and I really enjoy it, I do . . ."

"Good. I'm glad."

"But it must be pricey. I don't know anything about stereos or what they cost, but that has to be at least several hundred dollars. And I just wonder where you got that kind of money."

"It wasn't all that expensive."

The stereo in fact had cost Paul $2,300, plus tax.

"But still. You never have any money and . . ." It crossed Hunter's mind that Paul must think he was implying theft or embezzlement or . . . what?

Paul was thinking the same.

They sat, frozen in silence.

"What is this stuff, anyhow?" Hunter said, tapping his plate with his fork. "What do you call it?"

"It's American chop suey."

"Macaroni? Hamburg? Tomato something?"

"And spices."

"I'm getting better at this blind business. It's true what they say; the other senses do begin to compensate."

Silence.

"I've been listening to the preachers. On the radio. There are any number of these people, salesmen, and they preach and rant and promise miraculous healing; and then they say, 'Send your money to Brother Heartache today—for Jesus' sake—and your heart will never ache again. Ay-men. Ay-men.' It's fascinating. Black comedy."

Silence. "I sold some stuff," Paul said. Hunter made no response. "I sold some of my sculptures, in the show, and that's where I got the money."

"Some? More than one?"

"Yes."

"But they weren't . . . done. This is incredible. There wasn't a single piece that you could say . . . The show was . . ."

"I know."

"And you *sold* these things?" Hunter felt accused, insulted. "How much did you make?"

"Seven thousand."

Hunter said nothing.

"I sold them. It seemed all right to."

Hunter looked at him accusingly. Then he rose from the table and made his way to his room. He did not come out again that night.

.   .   .

For nearly a week they were silent. Hunter refused to speak. Paul, hurt and angry, was unable to. His sense of obligation had turned to rage and then to pity.

One night at dinner Paul was astonished to hear himself say in an anguished voice, "I'm *trying,* Hunter. I *want* to be a better sculptor, you know."

"The pieces were not finished. The work was not done."

Paul wanted to say that his work was as finished as he could make it *now.* He was young yet and still had time to learn. He had not betrayed Hunter by having this small success. But he forced himself to say only, "No. You're right."

In a new tone, cool, objective, Hunter said, "Well, at least you made money."

"Yes."

"And got commissions?"

"Let me get you some coffee."

"There *were* commissions?"

"Yes."

"For what? How many?"

"The political pieces. The Eisenhower, the Lincoln, the two Kennedys, the whole series."

"You don't have a series. You told them you did?"

"I told them I would."

"Well, well, " Hunter said. "*That* means money."

"But I'm trying, Hunter. I try to remember your critiques. I try to find the mystery in the piece, the secret lines, and I keep reminding myself about the dangers of deliberate obscurity, and I know . . ."

"What does it matter, Paul." Hunter gave him a terrible smile. "You're on your way to being rich."

Paul's pity for Hunter turned to loathing.

Again, as always, Hunter rose and left the table.

.   .   .

Hunter lay on his bed and shuddered. So. It had happened. Paul had money and would have more. He could leave now at any time. He hated Paul for helping him. He hated him for having money.

He pulled his knees to his chest and locked his arms around them. Without making a sound, he screamed as loud and as long as he could. At the end, he was covered with sweat, exhausted, but he had managed to pull back from despair and settle into simple, manageable hatred.

"God damn you, Paul Bates," he said. "God damn you. God damn you." It was a soothing sound.

.   .   .

"Physiologically," Dr. Forrest said, "there is no reason why you can't see. You have scar tissue and you always will, but the mechanism for sight is there. You should be able to see right now." He was being patient. "Do you see? I mean, do you?"

Hunter said, "If I had my sight . . ."

Dr. Forrest waited through a long silence. "Perhaps you'll begin to see," he said, "once you've decided that's what you want." Dr. Forrest bit his lip, determined to outwait this maddening, self-indulgent, willful man. "There's not much to be said for darkness, you know." He continued waiting. He waited some more. "My God, you're impossible," he said.

Hunter said nothing.

• • •

Hunter sat alone in the living room, his head thrown back, waiting. The Thai cleaning woman had left. Paul would not be in for hours yet. There was nothing to do but wait. For what? He felt for the radio and pushed the automatic setting for the funniest preacher station. The volume was too high and at once the room was filled with Brother Gabriel's unctuous voice:

> O sing to the Lord a new song,
> for he has done marvelous things!

Hunter punched the OFF button.

• • •

Paul had had enough of this whimsical, tyrannical, hateful old man. He was loathsome. He was detestable.

That night as Paul lay in bed chewing over the cruel things he could say to the old bastard, a great feeling of calm came upon him. He would get out. Leave. He would hire somebody to look after Hunter and look after the house and then he'd take off. Sayonara, Hunter.

He woke up feeling calm after a good night's sleep. He lay in bed for a while, a little frightened at his decision but determined to go through with it. How good it would be to fuck around when he felt like it, to have a girl beside him again, to live his own life, to *work,* for Christ's sake. He got out of bed singing. He showered and threw on his jeans and tee shirt and, a little sobered by the thought of telling Hunter, he left the studio to go over to the house and start making breakfast.

He had just begun cracking eggs when the doorbell rang. A fat woman with short blond hair stood on the doorstep, a suitcase by her side. She smiled at him, and her smile was so warm and so friendly that it caught him completely off guard.

"You must be Paul Bates," she said. "I'm Rachel."

4

Three months passed and Paul Bates had still not told Hunter he was leaving. Things went on as they were, with only small changes in the routine of the days. Rachel made breakfast for Hunter and then disappeared upstairs to write or, more often, into the studio to complete her catalogue of Hunter's work. Sometimes Paul straggled in as Rachel was finishing the breakfast dishes and then all three of them would sit down and have coffee. The Thai cleaning woman came in mid-morning, made Hunter's lunch at noon, and sometimes put together a casserole that Paul could stick into the oven and have for dinner. Rachel didn't eat meals herself—in the morning she had diet bread and in the evening a bowl of grains, as she called it—and so she saw no reason to cook, though she gladly made Hunter's breakfast. At night they sometimes watched television together, but mostly they went their own ways; that is, Hunter stayed in the living room and listened to his stereo, Paul slouched off to the studio for a little more work, and Rachel disappeared upstairs, where she carried on her own mysterious existence. That existence in-

cluded a prie-dieu, a plain wooden crucifix, and a picture
machine that she used for writing. It also included many boxes
of Belgian chocolates. This much Hunter had learned from
the cleaning woman and it had been confirmed by Rachel
herself, with the additional information that the picture machine was an IBM PC, but exactly what she was writing, and
why, she would not say. She was pleasant, energetic, and
intensely secretive. And, according to the cleaning woman,
she was fat.

Though Hunter was still alone with his stereo for the
greater part of his day, he had companionship and conversation and, at the best of times, the odd but comfortable
feeling that he was the favorite child in a loving family. He
feared only that this would end, that Paul would want a life
of his own and would leave him, or that Rachel would complete the catalogue of his work and would leave him. Or that
Paul and Rachel would fall in love with each other and leave
him. And that he would be alone once more and in the dark.

.   .   .

They were sitting at the breakfast table, the three of them;
it was one of those mornings. The sun was pouring in and a
bird was singing in the shrubs outside the window and Hunter
felt that, if only they stayed this way forever, everything
would be all right. But then Rachel got up and left the table,
pausing at the door just long enough to say she expected to
finish the catalogue this morning. "What?" Hunter shouted.
"I'm nearly done," she called back to him, as the screen door
slammed behind her and she crossed the lawn to the studio.
Hunter caught his breath because, with the slamming of that
door, he knew the end was about to begin.

"Hunter?" Paul said. "I want to ask you a favor. I need
some help."

"Oh? Packing?" He could turn surly in an instant.

"Oh, for Christ's sake, come off it."

"Are you finally going to leave?"

"Is that what you want?" Paul said. "Do you want me to leave?"

"Oh, just go. Why don't you just go. You've got plenty of money. You've got *commissions*. You've got *time,* now that Rachel's here." And he added, hollowly, "You've got your vision."

"Yes, I can see, and you can't," Paul said. "Poor you. You're *blind*."

"Don't."

"It's been over a year now and you haven't let up once: bitching and moaning and snapping my head off. You're blind and I'm not. Tough shit, Hunter. But I'm not taking any more."

Hunter sat, waiting.

"Now, I need your help. I want you to come out to the studio and take a look at my new piece. You can feel it. You'll know what it needs."

"I don't want to talk about it."

"It needs something. I don't know what to do next."

"I'm not talking about it. I won't."

"You will. It's Abraham and Isaac. I'm doing it. But it's yours, and I need some help."

.   .   .

Rachel completed the catalogue that morning, and it was not just a title list of individual works, but a complete descriptive catalogue with dates of inception and completion, along with whatever exhibit history each piece might have. That afternoon she printed it out on her computer, and at dinnertime she placed the heavy stack of paper in Hunter's hands.

"Look," she said, excited and happy at having finished it at last. "Isn't this terrific, Hunter? This is all *your* work. Heft it. Feel how heavy? Paul, look."

"Why bother?" Hunter said.

"Well, you have to be just a *little* proud. *I* am, and I only catalogued it."

"Burn it," he said.

"Do you see? Now do you see?" Paul said. "That's how he is with me all the time."

"Hunter, I'm sorry that you're blind," Rachel said. "I am, truly. But I didn't do it to you and I won't allow you to abuse me for it." And she added, almost as an afterthought, "You certainly do take the joy out of things."

"Ha!" Hunter said, and sat through the meal in silence.

 .   .   .

"I am crushed with shame. I am brought low among sinners. I have sinned against you, my Lord, and I repent. I repent." For a long moment nothing but choked sobs came from the stereo, the hysterical weeping of the true professional, Hunter thought. "I have sinned against my family. I have sinned against my friends. I have sinned against the good Christian people throughout the world who look to me and who depend upon me and upon my sacred mission." There were more sobs, somewhat less professional. Listening carefully, Hunter could count the beats. And then, right on cue: "But I have carried the weight of my sin to the top of Calvary, and I have repented, and I have been forgiven. Oh, blessed Jesus, what a weight I have borne. And I have borne it all! I have carried it all! Jesus Christ, sitting on the right hand of God, says that he has washed the sinner clean. The blood of Jesus has washed away my sins and I am clean once more, and whole, and I have returned to my mission of saving souls for the Kingdom. Glory be to God for his great mercy! Glory be to God for the cleansing blood of Jesus! The blood of Jesus! The blood of Jesus is not a medicine. It is a cure! It's settled! The agony is over! Glory be to God, I'm pure again."

It was midafternoon and Rachel had come downstairs for a break from her writing. She stood and listened in disbelief as Hunter called out Amen Amen and laughed in a way she had never heard before. It was bitter laughter, filled with hate.

. . .

Hunter's eyesight returned so dimly, so gradually, that at first he was not aware he could see. He got up one morning much earlier than usual and felt his way to the bathroom. He showered and did his teeth, and as he stood before the mirror to shave, he realized that something had changed. The motes of light that crazed the surface of this eyes had been replaced by a barely perceptible image. He studied that image for a long moment and found he was looking at his own face.

"Rachel!" he shouted. "Rachel! Paul!" Hunter walked quickly to the kitchen, moving for the first time without his blind shuffle, but Rachel was not there. It was too early.

He went back to the bathroom and examined his face. He could not see well enough to make out the tiny seams that extended across his nose from cheek to cheek, but he could see the creases on either side of his mouth where they had sewed his torn face back together. It didn't look bad. It looked as if he were about to smile. "Rachel!" he said softly. But even as he said it, he saw what would happen. Now they would surely leave him.

An hour later Rachel came down to make breakfast, and Paul—early for once—came in from the studio at just the same time. They found Hunter sitting in the living room next to the stereo, his head cocked slightly in that listening attitude he had acquired since the accident.

. . .

"I've gone as far as I can," Paul said. "It's roughed out, but I can't go ahead without your help."

"What are you talking about?" Hunter said.

"The Abraham and Isaac. I followed your clay model and I've done all the pointing up. It's perfectly in scale, but I've never worked marble this big before."

"Is this *her* idea? It is, isn't it."

"It's not her idea." Silence. "I need your advice. I'm ready to carve and I could make a fatal blunder."

A month had passed since Hunter's sight had returned.

"It's *your* work. I'll never lay claim to it. It's yours. So you'd better look it over."

"I'm *blind,*" Hunter said.

.   .   .

Another month had passed, each day the same.

Rachel appeared for breakfast and disappeared up to her room for the rest of the day, except for her afternoon trips for pastry. When she reappeared for her odd dinner—a bowl of grains and two slices of diet bread—she was as provokingly cheery as ever.

Paul worked each morning and night in the studio, but he did not ask for help and he did not mention the statue again. He had that crazy look about him that meant he was working well.

Every day Hunter grew more curious about what went on upstairs from morning till night and, more to the point, what was going on in the studio. And every day he had to concentrate harder on looking blind.

.   .   .

Paul had left for class and Hunter was listening to *The Art of the Fugue,* but he could not concentrate. His mind was racing. His head ached. He was determined he would not go to the studio and spy on Paul Bates's work. He pushed the button for the preacher station.

"Our God is a fearsome God . . ."

"You're telling me," Hunter said.

". . . a God of power and might. The Holy Bible tells us

the story of King David when he brought the Ark of the Covenant to Jerusalem. Now the Ark of the Covenant . . ."

"I'm going to make some tea," Rachel said, coming into the room. "Care for some?"

Hunter started and said, "My God, don't go sneaking up on me like that," and he punched the OFF button on the stereo.

"Oh no," Rachel said, "leave it on. He's going to tell about David dancing. I love that story."

"Do you *know* the story?" Hunter said. It was a challenge.

"I just told you, I love it." She ran the water for tea and then returned to him.

"Well, go read it again," Hunter said, "because it's not the lovable story you think. It's about the great destroyer."

"Tell," she said, sitting by his side, and looking.

He cleared his throat. He needed to be asked again.

"Tell, Hunter," she said. "Come on."

"It's in the Book of Samuel," he said. "Or Samuel Two." He had to be careful not to catch her eye. "Anyhow, the Ark was being borne into the city on an ox cart, and David was dancing in front of it, and everybody was cheering and yelling and carrying on. But all of a sudden one of the oxen stumbled and the cart began to tip. To keep the Ark from falling— because it was so sacred it could never be allowed to touch the ground—some poor Israelite bastard put up his hand to steady it and, without meaning to, he touched the Ark with a single finger and . . . do you know what happened?" Rachel just kept listening. "And immediately, *instantly,* God struck him dead."

"What a wonderful story!"

"Wonderful? It's a story about God as mean, whimsical, tyrannical, hateful, vicious. . . "

"Unfair."

"What?"

"Blindingly unfair."

"Exactly," Hunter said. "Well, you get my point."

And then, together, they laughed.

Rachel got the tea and poured it and set a box of chocolates between them. "Have a choc," she said, "I absolutely live on them." And after a while she said, "How long have you been able to see, Hunter?"

.   .   .

"Blindness was never your problem, Hunter," Rachel said. "It's God."

It was the day after she'd told him they knew he could see—yes, Paul knew too; they had known for some time— and Hunter was feeling exposed and betrayed. The intimacy of their tea talk yesterday had been replaced by a new terror that they would leave him now and by a new fury against the God who had destroyed his life.

"You've become obsessed by God," Rachel said, "and in a very unhealthy way, too."

"Leave me alone," Hunter said, in one of his black moods. "And stop talking to me about God."

"It's those programs you listen to, Hunter. They're designed to make any thinking person a little crazy."

"And don't bother praying for me!"

"I don't pray for you, Hunter. I pray for strength."

This brought him up short. "Why don't you leave and just be done with me," he said softly, his voice barely a whisper.

"Paul is leaving," she said. "He can't finish the sculpture. He's given up."

.   .   .

They were in the studio, finally, all three of them. Rachel and Paul were looking at Hunter while Hunter looked at the roughed-out work. It was indeed his Abraham and Isaac, but done by a different hand.

Paul had worked from Hunter's small clay model. In both,

the boy was stretched across the sacrificial stone. In both, the father bent over him—eyes averted, knife poised—ready to strike. The clay model, a little cracked and hardened to stone, still possessed an inhabiting spirit, a life of its own.

Standing next to it, exactly five times its size, Paul's marble sculpture was a scene of wild barbarity. He had caught the hand on the knife, the knife poised to strike, the father's terrible obedient anguish and the son's surrender. But it was incomplete, unborn, as if the work itself were still struggling out of the stone and into life.

Hunter mounted the platform on which the sculpture stood and gazed at it, transfixed. It was bold and daring. It had integrity. It had passion. Despite the roughness of the work and the missed opportunities within the stone, this Abraham and Isaac revealed the talent he had once believed in. Paul had it after all. Paul Bates was the real thing. Hunter hated him more than ever.

The silence in the room went on and on.

When he could stand it no longer, Paul said, "It's yours, Hunter. Do what you want with it."

With his finger Hunter traced the old man's brow, his hooded eyes.

"You can complete it, Hunter. Reshape it. You can just carve away everything that isn't your Abraham and Isaac."

Hunter turned and stared down on him. Paul stared back.

"Or you can destroy it, if you want. It's yours."

Hunter traced the knifeblade with his finger. "It's very good," he said.

"It's yours."

"Though of course there are problems, Paul."

For a long time they looked at the sculpture and then, like conspirators, they looked at each other.

Rachel folded her hands and said nothing.

Hunter stooped and picked up the hammer and chisel that

lay at the base of the statue. He raised the chisel, holding it poised in the air, like Abraham's knife. He turned and looked at Paul. Paul looked back.

"It's mine?" Hunter said.

Hunter placed the chisel firmly against Abraham's brow. He raised the hammer and held it there, poised to strike.

"No," Rachel said, a whisper.

Paul turned, done with it all, and went up the stairs to pack.

Rachel raised a hand to her mouth. In her mind, the great destroyer brought the hammer down hard, shattering the old man's brow and eyes and chin. There was a crackling sound as marble sheared from marble. The face. The hands. In her mind, the hammer clanged again and again, vengeful, destructive, returning blow for blow.

And still Hunter stood there, motionless, poised to strike.

Rachel spoke then, her voice astonishing and calm. "Come down, Hunter," she said. "Just let it be."

Hunter lowered his arms to his sides and rested his head, aching, against Paul's statue.

"That's good," she said, feeling herself begin to breathe again. "That's very good." She busied herself, in her fat practical way, getting a tarp and covering the statue with it—"Give me a hand here, Hunter; that's right"—and tying it in around the bottom, talking sensibly all the while, calling him back from his madness. "We'll just let it stand here," she said, "and take up a little space. Paul will send for it eventually, don't you think? He'll want to work on it. Or it'll just sit here and get old. And that's all right too."

Hunter stood listening. It was good to hear the sound of her calm and competent voice and to surrender to her ordinary words.

"This is better, isn't it," she said. "It's only in melodrama that sculptors take a hammer to their work. Real life just isn't like that." She finished covering the statue and wiped her hands on a tee shirt lying there. "That should do," she said. She cast an eye around the studio, an automatic gesture, to make sure everything was in place. Everywhere on shelves along the wall stood the witness to Hunter's life work, all of it numbered, described, and now carefully shrouded. She turned away quickly, though as she did she caught a glimpse— on a shelf just above the door—of the elegant ebony feet of the dog Anubis, guardian of the necropolis.

She put her arm through Hunter's and started out of the studio. "In real life, people get mad and fight like hell and then they have a cup of tea and just get on with it. Come on," she said, "we'll pretend this is real life, Hunter, and I'll make us a cup of tea. Tea and chocs. There's nothing like it."

5

Years back, when Rachel left him, she had been an intelligent, responsible, academic wife with a good figure and a good mind. If she stole things from dinner parties, it was just her way of dealing with unhappiness. If she had intentionally damaged each of his sculptures, it was because she felt used by him and was paying him back for it. He understood this, and anyhow the damage was minimal. *She* was what mattered to him. *She* was the only thing he cared about.

Hunter was proud that his blindness had led to this new clarity of vision. He could at last see his wife as another person, a woman with desires and needs and frustrations, and not just an adjunct of himself. He was going to do things differently this time, be a new and better husband to her. Already, just to please her, he had agreed to teach a small seminar on contemporary painting. It would get him out of the house and get him back into university life, she said, though, to tell the truth, she had implied that unless he did it, she'd leave. So once again he had art books spread out all over the place—for ideas, for inspiration, but mostly because this academic mess reminded him of the good old days with Rachel. And of course he'd given up listening to the preachers. They belonged to his blind period, they were a symptom of his depression, and for that reason, he had no interest in them any longer. He wanted to go back to the time when he and Rachel were first married, but with this difference: he would be the perfect husband; she would be the perfect wife.

Never mind, at least for now, that she refused to live with him as husband and wife. Or to explain where she had been or what she had done during those years away. Or even to tell him what she was writing each day at her preposterous IBM PC. And don't even think of the fat! and that hair!

All this aside, Hunter found himself obsessed by something mysterious in her that was not there before; he wanted to know and possess it, whatever it was. He loved her. He needed her. And now that she was with him once again, he would convince her to stay. He was determined to win her back, for good.

But Rachel had other loves and other needs and she was equally determined to leave him. For good.

· · ·

"Why, pray, do you eat that stuff?" Hunter was making conversation.

"The bread is high in fiber and low in calories. The grains are very nutritious. It's all part of my diet."

Diet indeed. Hunter didn't push it, knowing that silence or an argument lay ahead. It was November, one of those rare New England days when the air is sharp and the sun is high and you feel you can do anything at all. Hunter was determined to get things back on a normal plane with her no matter what it cost him.

"Tell me about your diet," he said.

Rachel looked at him for a moment and decided he was not just making fun. "Well, it's a joke diet, really," she said, "but it suits me just fine."

He was listening.

"I have my bread and grains in the morning and then just the grains at night—that's two hundred sixty calories plus one hundred eighty calories; so, four hundred forty altogether—and that way I can snack all day long, and of course sometimes I binge on salad or on veg."

"So it's the chocolates . . .?"

"That make me fat? Well, the chocolates when I'm writing, plus the pastries at Douce France in the afternoon when I'm not writing and the oat biscuits when the writing isn't going well, so you see it all adds up. But as I say, Hunter, it suits me fine."

"But you don't mind being . . .?"

"Fat? Of course I mind, that's why I diet. If I had regular meals *plus* all those treats, I'd be big as a house."

"But if you *had* regular meals, perhaps you wouldn't *want* all those treats."

"Oh, poor Hunter. That's just who I am."

He decided to push it just a little further. "And the hair?"

"Who knows," she said. "A folly. It struck me one day that fat women who look like me always have a mop of bleached hair, so I thought I'd give it a try. And it suits me. It strikes at the roots of vanity."

"Some people might think it's self-hatred."

She lifted her eyebrows at him. "But not you, Hunter. You're too smart for that. You know how tricky a thing self-hatred is."

"Are you implying something about *me?*" She'd changed, he could see that, and not for the better. Why did he feel that he loved her now more than ever before?

Rachel simply gazed at him with her new and disconcerting

calm, but before he could react, in came the Thai cleaning woman, Lon Chi, in her black smock and little black slippers. Rachel greeted her with exaggerated warmth—to infuriate him, no doubt—and Hunter, refusing to let on he noticed, threw a satisfied smile in their direction and went to his study to prepare his seminar.

. . .

A week went by. Lon Chi, the cleaning woman, ducked into Hunter's study for the third time that morning and waited just long enough to be noticed before she started her routine of bowing and smiling and saying she was sorry to interrupt.

"What is it you want?" Hunter said, but she just kept on smiling. "Do you want to clean in here?"

"Dust," she said. "Thank you."

Hunter tried to concentrate on an *Artforum* essay entitled "The Business of Art," but his new thick spectacles were causing him trouble and the essay was wrong-headed and programmatic and he was aware every minute of the presence of this little Thai woman who, to his mind, spent altogether too much time chatting with Rachel. Still, what you can't get around, you make use of, and so he said to her, "I see that you are very friendly with my wife."

"Yes, please. She is fine lady."

"What do you two talk about all the time? I just wonder."

"Very fine lady."

"Does she tell you things? What does she tell you?"

Lon Chi turned away, blushing, seized by shyness or some misdirected sense of propriety.

Hunter turned back to "The Business of Art."

Lon Chi worked in silence for some time, dusting around the room until she arrived again at his desk. She looked at him then, and said, "You have many books, but none of lady's books."

"What about her books?" he said. "Tell me."

"Flambeau books," she said. "Very fine."

.   .   .

Hunter, in his months of pretended blindness, had managed to discover that Rachel was writing some kind of novel. The characters had names like Alison and Brad and Max, and they did an unusual amount of talking, but Hunter's desire to spy was always curtailed by his fear of being caught, and so he had no idea what the novel was about, but his guess was that it had no great future.

In fact, he was both right and wrong. Rachel was at work on her twelfth novel of love and passion—a Flambeau Romance by Victoria Heath—and though its future was not great by any standard Hunter would recognize, it was great indeed to the thousands of Victoria Heath devotees who bought and read and sighed over each Flambeau as it appeared.

Rachel had never read one of these things until she landed a job as receptionist in a makeshift publishing house that produced Candlelight, Torchlight, Sunset, Hurricane, and Tornado romances. They were published one-a-week, and they were written by a small band of women and men who were practical, dedicated wage earners. What surprised Rachel most about these writers was their sincerity; they were serious about producing good books—quickly written and quickly read, without any moral deviation to upset the reader. They liked what they were doing. They were proud of it. They knew they were practicing a wifey-mothery form of fiction, but it was fiction nonetheless, and what was wrong with wives and mothers anyhow? In their own way, they were creating literature.

Rachel answered the phone and took messages and, during the long stretches of inactivity, she read these ghastly books. Eventually she came to see that, like all rotten art, these books sprang from innocent longings and ministered to the starved mind, the hungry heart, the unawakened sensibility. They seemed to her then a kind of pornography of the soul, and for a while she would have nothing to do with them and came near to quitting her job, but as she got to know the writers well, she saw they were all engaged in a harmless enterprise: creating a world of easy, faithful, satisfying love that nobody could take seriously for even a moment. She herself had spent a year in just such a search—a hard, messy, painful year that changed her life forever—and she had sympathy for their immortal longings. In an odd way, she decided, it was *their* search for God. Or was that going too far?

Eventually, half as a joke, she wrote one of these romance novels, *Love's Victims,* under the name of Victoria Heath. It was a phenomenal success. In her hands the romance formula took on some kind of magic that readers responded to by purchasing her books in record numbers. No one seemed bothered by her gentle irony. No one seemed to notice her subversive commentary on the permanence of love. She wrote another, *Love Triumphant,* and it too was a great success. For her third novel, *Love and Friendship,* the publishers doubled her advance, named her books the Flambeau Romances, and printed her name—Victoria Heath—in letters slightly larger than the title. She wrote four of these a year. They were the secret behind her blond hair and her fat, and the secret too behind that hominess and calm that Hunter found so disconcerting.

Because whatever it was she seemed to be doing in writing these books, Rachel was not attempting to create literature of any kind whatsoever. She was simply rearranging life in this world the way it ought to be—with a gentle, ironic nod toward rectifying God's mistakes.

∎   ∎   ∎

Lon Chi—or Linda as she'd now become for the past few weeks—was loitering again in Hunter's study. She wore red Adidas and jeans and Hunter noticed, not for the first time, that she was really very pretty. She couldn't be more than thirty.

"And how is the family?" Hunter said. He always took the roundabout route in pumping her for information.

"Very fine family, thank you," she said, bowing and smiling and bowing again.

Why on earth did she want to be called Linda if she intended to go through life bowing and smiling, Hunter thought, unaware that he was smiling back in just the same way.

"Thank you," she said again.

"And your husband? Is he still working two jobs?"

"Husband has bought dry cleaners for which we save. Very fine for us, thank you."

"He's bought a dry cleaning shop? Good God! And how long have you been in this country? Two years?"

"We are here five years. It is very fine for us."

Thirty years old. Immigrants with nothing at all. Not even speaking the language, and now they owned a dry cleaning business. Simple determination could accomplish anything, he reflected, and by God he'd get Rachel *back*.

Linda mistook his blank stare as a request for more information. "You are my only house, thank you. I clean for you only. And I make lunch. Then I work in dry cleaners." She pointed upstairs. "Lady is very good for us."

"The lady is very good for everybody," he said, with just a trace of irony.

"Very romantic," she said. " 'They embraced at last and, for a moment that they thought would last forever, their two hearts beat as one.' " She blushed a wonderful rose color.

"You're reading her books?"

"I learn my English from them," she said.

"Well, *that* should prepare you for life in America," he said. On her way out of the room, Linda paused as if she had suddenly remembered the purpose of her visit. "You don't worry," she said. "I work for you until lady goes."

. . .

Hunter was determined to make Rachel stop this nonsense and just settle down here as his wife. He corrected himself: he was determined to *persuade* her logically, lovingly, that *she really wanted* to settle down here as his wife. He would listen. He would be responsive to her needs. And then he would get what he wanted.

They were seated at the table and Hunter had still not worked out how he should proceed. He was trying to quiet his annoyance at the absurdity of the meal—he was having a Swanson's sole meunière he had zapped in the microwave and Rachel was having her bowl of grains—when suddenly it occurred to him that this was all a fantasy, a nightmare. He was a distinguished academic, a former sculptor of some reputation, and he had let himself become a spy and a sneak and a beggar in the attempt to persuade this fat, silly woman to act like his wife. And she was *already* his wife! She had obligations! He choked on his sole then, and after a little coughing fit, he took a sip of wine and smiled weakly.

"A bone," he said, "in the fish."

"In a frozen dinner? I doubt that."

She'd become such a know-it-all.

"More likely it's indignation you choked on."

He would let this, too, pass unremarked.

"Sorry," she said.

"I read *The Last Caress* today. You're Victoria Heath, aren't you."

"Yes, of course."

"Of course? Why didn't you tell me? I asked you repeatedly what it was you were working on up there."

"I knew you'd think it stupid, Hunter, and I just didn't see what good could come from your . . . *reviling* my work."

"I wouldn't *revile* it. I don't *revile* things."

Rachel laughed.

"It's very badly written, of course. I suppose they all are. The whole genre."

"They're fun," she said.

"But you *can* write well. What first attracted me to you was the quality of your mind and your ability to handle the written word."

"And my admiration for you."

"Yes, *yes*. But if you *can* write well, why don't you? I mean, why don't you write a real novel? A work of art."

"If I wrote a real novel, it wouldn't be a work of art, at least not in your terms."

"And why not, pray?"

"Because it wouldn't be formulaic. It wouldn't have a tidy plot where all the parts come together, perfectly dovetailed, to produce a surprising—but, mind you, inevitable—resolution. You call it art, Hunter. I call it formula."

He was staring at her in astonishment. Did she for one second think that those damned Flambeau things were *not* formulaic? He was, literally, speechless.

"A real novel, if I were to write one, would try to capture the randomness, the sprawl, the . . . well, the messiness of life. There would be no causal thread running through it— you know, because you *did* this, *that* happened—and there'd be no tiny cast of characters recurring in a set pattern, as if our lives took place on a stage where all the small parts have to be played by the same three or four actors, and there'd be no recurring images to tell the professors what the novel *really* was about. It would be chaos, and a wanton waste of everything good and valuable, and heartbreak that came from standing inside the only skin you will ever really know. There would be nothing to hold it together except the person it was about and . . ."

But instead of going on, she scooped up another spoonful of those damned grains and just looked at him.

"And?" he said. "Yes?"

"And a single tiny thin *thin* thread of God's meddling in our lives."

She let the grains trickle back into the bowl.

"Yes?"

"That's what would hold it together. That would be the only reality. The rest is madness anyhow."

He had no idea what she was talking about.

. . .

Rachel had left Hunter in the first place not because of what he was or did, and not because of Blackie's spiteful little insight, but because suddenly she had seen a vision of herself—dead, without ever having lived. She was not sure what that vision was supposed to mean, but she knew she had to get away and she knew she had to find . . . something. She decided to look for love.

Like Hunter, she began with sex, but unlike him, she did not use liquor as a lubricant or an excuse. She was a good-looking woman of forty-one who dressed well and was on the make, and she had no trouble finding all the men she wanted. She lived comfortably from her joint checking account with Hunter—she had earned it, after all—and since she did not work, she was available at any time of day or night.

It had been easy to get started. She went where she was most comfortable—to an art show—and she wore black satin, cut low, and looked available. She spent that night with a stockbroker whose wife was away, and didn't understand him in any case, and from the stockbroker she drifted from man to man.

There were gifts, dinners, mid-morning assignations, lunch, late lunch, before and after lunch, and always sex. She enjoyed it, or at least participated fully, doing what was asked, asking things she had never dreamed about. "Do it," she would say, "do it, do it," and she would moan with pleasure the way they liked, the way that made them harder, fiercer, penetrating to her core, spilling semen in her mouth, her womb, her anal tract, it didn't matter where. "Love," she would say, "oh, my love," even as she recognized that love had nothing to do with it, and smiled her secret smile, because it was all a game, and nobody got hurt, and what did it matter after all.

And when the morning came—or sodden afternoons, or dusk, or any time when it was done and over—an emptiness possessed her like a tomb, and she was dead again, and lay there staring into the dark. It was a hard, cold, painful year and it ended, as it began, in bed.

He was one of her nearly anonymous lovers, a friend of an acquaintance, and he was so polite and courtly and sexually unpromising that Rachel thought he must be gay. He was short and skinny, with thick glasses and a wide thin mouth. He looked to her like an accountant whose idea of a wild time would be a disco and a carriage ride through Central Park. When he invited her to his apartment for a drink, she expected him to offer her coffee, and indeed he did, followed by a line of cocaine and some funny pills he took just before they moved into the bedroom. It was very late at night, and Rachel had spent a good part of the afternoon with another man, in another bed, and she was not prepared for the stamina and sheer staying power of this new skinny little lover. At first she was relieved that he brought her to orgasm—she wouldn't have to fake it or go away only half done—but when he continued on and on, and so did she, she began to wish he would just wind it up and come. "Come," she whispered to him, "I want you to, now, now," and she did the things that had always worked in the past, but still he held on and on and on, pushing and grinding, and she was hurting, badly, and she knew she had to stop him so she whispered, "Please, please," and he said, "Are you ready? Are you ready for it?" He suddenly drove deeper into her, and as he did, he rolled to the side and reached one hand up to the nightstand. He grabbed a capsule that was in the ashtray and cracked it between his teeth. He snapped the thing in half and inhaled deeply. His face contorted, as if he were in agony, and he said, "Christ, oh Jesus fucking Christ," and he froze in position: his back arched, his teeth clenched, for a half minute he stopped breathing, and then he let out a long high shout as, finally, he came. He collapsed on top of her. They were covered in sweat, soaking, breathless. They lay, silent, for a long time.

Rachel was emptied out, used up. This was not just the usual fatigue that followed sex; it was a kind of terminal exhaustion she had felt before; an entombment; a living death. Something had happened to her in that moment between asking him to stop and his reaching for that capsule. Something had happened in her brain, or in her soul—she was sure of that—and nothing would ever be the same. She slept, and when she woke, it was almost dawn. She could see a pale light beyond the window and, incredibly, she could hear a bird singing.

She recognized it then: a thin *thin* line that threaded a childhood breakfast to a stolen silver spoon to a vision in Hunter's studio to a moment in this very bed. She saw it leading forward to . . . but then the line was lost to her.

"Again?" he said, his eyes brilliant and blind without his

glasses, his hands already moving on her body. "No, I'm done for tonight," she said, and though she did not know it, she was nearly done for all the nights to come. She would go back to him once, and back to other lovers once or twice, because sex was a need of hers, and it was good, and it satisfied some part of her. But not all of her. And not the part she cared most about. This life was over.

In the morning she said to him, "I need a job. Do you know how I can get a job?" He introduced her to Campagna at the makeshift publishing company; Campi shrugged and said he had nothing to offer except Receptionist. She took it.

She wrote *Love's Victims* and had a good time doing it, and then—for the blessed quiet of the place—she went to the guest house of an Anglican convent and there she wrote another, and another.

She asked to join the convent as a nun, though she knew that as a Roman Catholic and a married woman there was no hope of that, but they were sympathetic and let her stay on as a permanent paying guest. She followed the convent Rule, attending Mass and Evensong and meditating on the life of Christ and the Christian mysteries, and in her free time she wrote her books and dieted and bleached her hair.

She would have spent her life this way. But when she heard about Hunter, very late in his blindness, she left the guest house of the Convent of Saint John and went to Boston intending to care for him until he died. But then his sight returned.

She was waiting now for him to set her free.

.   .   .

Linda arrived dressed in her old black smock and her little black slippers. Her hair was done up in a Thai knot of some sort and she was wearing exaggerated makeup.

"I give a talk at children's school," she explained, "straight after I make you lunch."

"But why the get-up?" Hunter said. "Why are you dressed this way?"

"Cross-cultural education." Linda laughed and made an exaggerated bow. "Is Halloween too. Very fine."

For the first time, Hunter wondered if she had been making fun of him all these months.

. . .

"You tell her things so she'll tell me, don't you," Hunter said.

And Rachel said, "How clever do you think I am?"

. . .

Hunter had long since abandoned the effort to penetrate that mystery concealed in Rachel, whatever it was. At this point he just wanted her to stay. He had tried reasoning, arguing, accusing, denouncing, and threatening. He had tried gifts, and patience, and asking, and listening, and no-strings loving. None of it had worked.

He had done his best to change, to be a larger man, to be a better husband. He tried to listen more carefully, to be more generous with his understanding, to give her a sense of complete freedom *here,* in Boston, so she wouldn't be hankering after some convent in upstate New York. Moreover, he had not pressed her for sex, not even once. They lived like a couple of virgins, she upstairs, he down. And still she did not see that he had changed, that he'd become another person. For *her.*

What would it take to make her feel both at home and free? What? And even as he asked the question, he had the answer. She would always want to get away. It had nothing to do with him.

For a moment, he wished there was a God. He was desperate enough to pray.

. . .

It was early December and colder than any year in Boston history. It was too cold even to snow. The house was cozy, though, and Hunter had just come into the kitchen to put on some coffee and to take a peek at how the movers were doing with the sculpture.

Repeatedly during the past month, Paul Bates had called and written and finally sent a telegram saying he wanted to do more work on the Abraham and Isaac, if Hunter was willing of course, and could he have it back? Hunter had hung up the phone, thrown away the letters, and it was only by accident that when the telegram arrived, it was Rachel who got it. As a favor to Rachel, then, Hunter had agreed to ship the sculpture to Paul. He had fitted the padded yokes to the figures and had braced them from above and from the sides, but it was Rachel who had made the arrangements and it was she who was supervising the move. Hunter had laid down one condition: that Bates simply not appear.

Hunter finished making the coffee and went to the side window to see how they were coming along. Four hefty men were doing some kind of balancing act with the boxed and padded sculpture as they tried to get it up on the tailgate of a big orange U-Haul. Rachel was there, bundled into an old Army coat, waving her hands and shouting directions. The problem, Hunter could see, was that all the weight rested on the two men in front. They were powerful, no doubt, but they didn't seem to understand the basic physics of lifting a huge unevenly balanced object. And then, against all probability, the crate stabilized and they slipped it smoothly onto the bed of the truck. Rachel applauded and they gave each other high-fives as if they had done something tricky and smart. Good God. And good riddance.

But here was another step toward Rachel's leaving him. Consciously, he listened to the clock ticking while he waited for Rachel to come in.

The kitchen door banged open. It was not Rachel but Linda who came in, her head and face concealed beneath a crimson ski mask, her body draped in a long fur coat. She was wearing Rachel's Blackglama mink which, on Linda's tiny body, hung right to the floor. Ten years earlier that coat had cost him over fifteen thousand dollars.

"I see you've got a new coat," Hunter said, and he surprised himself by sounding glad about it.

"From lady." Linda bowed to him as she took off her ski mask. And then, with that smile and with her bare face and still wearing the coat, she looked straight at him. "Lady is saint," she said and, before Hunter could respond, she added, "She convent lady."

Hunter felt his insides give way. He knew all about Rachel and the convent from going through her desk, reading her mail, listening on the phone extension.

He had to do something and he had to do it at once. He had tried everything but begging. It was a last resort and he was not above it. He would beg.

"I'm sorry we didn't call and let you know, Linda, but we're not going to need you today. So you don't have to work. You can go home. Or to the dry cleaners."

He would do his begging in private.

Linda frowned for a second and then said, "Okay, you busy with mover. I know." She put her crimson ski mask back on, adjusting it carefully around her eyes and nose. "You a saint too," she said. She bowed twice, and left.

. . .

"Rachel, we have to talk," he said.

She had brought the icy cold in with her and the blast of air had cleared his head and made him eager to get on with it.

"Well, wait till I get my things off. My, that was fun. I was sad to see it go, though. But, you see? I knew Paul would send for the sculpture. Artists never really leave their work unfinished. Right?"

"Rachel, please."

"Yes, Hunter, yes. Just let me get some coffee."

He stood at the counter, waiting.

"Those were awfully nice men, though I must say they're not very adept at handling sculpture. Did you see the size of them? Huge. I suppose that when you're that size, it never occurs to you that there's anything too heavy to . . ."

"Please!"

"All *right*," she said, and Hunter noticed with surprise that she was very nervous. She did not want this conversation.

"We have to talk about our life together. We have to talk about . . ." "Convent" was on his lips, but instead he cleared his throat and said, ". . . come over here and sit down."

They sat opposite each other at the kitchen table. He didn't know where to begin.

"Linda thinks you're a saint," he said, because it was the first thing that came to his mind. He made it sound like an accusation.

"I gave her my old coat. I loaned her money for the dry cleaning shop. Of course she thinks I'm a saint." She laughed, dismissing the question.

"You loaned her the money? I imagined you gave it."

"I did give it. But when you call it a loan, it's easier."

"You give away all your money, don't you."

"Yes."

"But you let *me* support you? Like a husband?"

"*After* I buy my grains and my candy. *I* pay for those."

"And the oat biscuits, I presume."

"No, Hunter. You pay for the oat biscuits. Like a husband."

He had been ready to beg and, suddenly, crazily, they were talking about who paid for biscuits.

"Oh, let's stop all this insanity about money and candy and those goddam biscuits. I don't care about biscuits. You can buy all the fucking biscuits from here to upstate New York."

His voice cracked in the middle of his anger. "I just want you to stay with me. I just . . . want you."

"Oh, Hunter," she said, and she too was near tears. "Please. Please don't."

"I just love you. I just want to love you."

"I know."

"I want you to love me. You used to love me. Is that so much to ask?"

"I do love you."

"But not the way you used to. Not the way I love you."

"Hunter." She stared down at her folded hands, but he said nothing and so she was forced to go on. "In every love affair, there's one person who loves more than the other. That's simply how things are. When we married, I loved you more. And now it's changed. You love me more than I love you."

"My God, you're a cold fish." He was furious. "Is that what love means to you? Is that what comes of being a self-pro-claimed expert on—capital R—Romance?"

"I'm sorry, Hunter. I truly am." She was crying now, mak-ing no sound. A single tear fell on her folded hands, and then another tear, and her face was wet with them, but still she only stared at him.

"Tears will get you nowhere," he said, though he was shaken by them.

"I loved you more, it's true. But all the same, I've never really been a good wife to you, Hunter. I never was."

"But you could be now," he said. "We could start over from here," and he reached out and covered her hands with his.

"It's too late now." She was speaking very gently. "I should have challenged you back then when we were first married. I should have fought for my life." She looked at him apol-ogetically. "I should have made you let me live."

"Just tell me what you *want! What* do you want? I'll give it. Anything. Only stay with me."

"I want to be free. Forgive me, but that's what I want."

"You are free."

"I want to be free . . . of you."

The room went red for a minute and then black and there was a horrible pain behind his eyes and Hunter hoped he was having a stroke. But his vision cleared and Rachel was still there, looking somehow beautiful and infuriating, and he said, "Then go. But before I'd pray to a God like yours, I'd choose damnation."

She went upstairs.

A quarter hour passed. Hunter sat in his study staring at a book on treasures of the Pharaohs, but he saw nothing. His mind was racing through the things he would say to her about her screwed-up concept of God and duty and love, especially love. What did she think? Where did she get these crazy ideas? Not to mention her ideas on *art.* He wanted right now to kill her, to crush her to death with his voice, with his words, with the illogic of everything she had said since coming home from that madhouse they were passing off as a convent.

An hour passed and he was exhausted and sick. He just wanted two things: he wanted to rest for a minute, only a minute, and he wanted Rachel. *Why* was she being so utterly unreasonable? *Why* was she determined to break his heart? And she would break his heart. He loved her that much. But did he love her enough to let her go?

"Oh, God help me," he said aloud, and smiled because he knew well that as soon as you messed around with God, he had you. The smile became a laugh, more ironic than bitter. And for a second he saw himself giving her the freedom she wanted, and he saw her leaving him, and he went hollow inside. Was he to be left with nothing? Nothing at all?

He went up the stairs to her room. He saw her there, in his imagination, kneeling at the prie-dieu, tall and slim and beautiful, profoundly grateful for his gift.

He knocked at her door, which was slightly ajar, and then he pushed it open with his finger. She was sitting at her computer, but facing him, a chocolate in her hand.

He had intended to say, in a soft and loving voice, "Go, Rachel, because I love you," but the sight of her fat body and the crazy halo of bleached hair and, dear God, the chocolate poised at her mouth . . . it all left him speechless. But she knew at a glance why he had come. She put down the chocolate and ran to his arms, saying "Oh, thank you, Hunter, thank you, thank you, thank you."

. . .

Linda gave Rachel a month's notice. They had bought a second dry cleaning shop, Linda explained, and her husband needed her to manage it. He didn't work very well without her. So this was her last week.

She had served them lunch—a thin soup and some godawful dish that looked like seaweed—and for once Hunter and Rachel sat down together to a more or less normal meal. Rachel hadn't given up her noon abstinence or her diet of bread and grains; she was eating lunch just to please Linda, and Hunter too of course.

"Delicious, Linda," Hunter said, as she cleared away the table. "I don't know how I'll manage without you."

"I send other girl for you. Very good and very smart Thai girl. She is working her way through college. She read every one of lady's books. She speaks English like a New Yorker."

"You're going to kill me with kindness," Hunter said.

"Just so long as you kill him," Rachel said. She too was leaving in a week and she intended to stop any sentimentality before it could start.

. . .

"But what about the crazy eating habits and the grains and all the rest of it? The chocolates?"

"That's just human baggage, Hunter, just another of Adam's wounds. Or, if you prefer, Eve's. It's a little better than stealing spoons."

"You *do* think you're a saint, don't you. You really are hell-bent on being holy."

"No, Hunter. You've got it backwards." Rachel shifted on the couch and pulled her legs up under her. Her hair had grown out, not to its original black but to a reddish-brown; it was short and very pretty. "Sanctity has nothing to do with this. You make me sound so smug. You make me feel I must *be* smug."

"But it *is* holiness that you're pursuing."

"No. Holiness is pursuing *me*."

Each evening now they sat in the living room and talked, much the way they had in their first years of marriage, except now they knew they had only days left together. Hunter had agreed to a separation, had volunteered a divorce—in case the Sisters should relent and allow her to become a nun—and he discovered that, having given her up, he now and then caught sight of that mystery in her that had so obsessed him. Whatever it was, it had something to do with why she was going or what she was going to.

"Holiness is pursuing you," he said. "My, my."

"Well, I know how it sounds. You can't talk about these things without sounding like an ass. That's why it's a mistake even to think about holiness or sanctity."

"Come again?"

"You can't take the temperature of your relationship with God."

"Why go away to a convent, then?"

"The guest house."

"Why go away to the guest house of a convent?"

"Oh, dear Hunter. Poor Hunter. Wonderful Hunter. I'm just trying to live my life. Responsibly. And do what I must."

"I see, for just a second, and then I don't see."

She thought for a long while and then said simply, "I don't know. I can't explain." Then instantly she said, "It's like this. Once when I was little—about five years old, I guess—I was with my parents and my uncle Frank, whom I adored, and we were all having breakfast at a little restaurant. It was at the beach and it was summer. He must have had a fruit salad or something with his breakfast because after we ate, they were all just chatting over coffee, and my uncle Frank looked over at me and raised his eyebrows, and then he flicked a watermelon seed at me. I don't know if it hit me or what, but I began to cry. And the strange thing is that I didn't know why I was crying. I didn't know *why*. Well, my uncle was very upset because he'd only been fooling, trying to be nice. And I was upset because I could see *he* was upset and so I began to cry even more. But I couldn't explain to anybody why I was crying, and to this day I don't know why I reacted like that to his flicking a little watermelon seed at me. I *knew* he was joking. I knew it was harmless. I didn't want to do it and yet I couldn't stop. I couldn't stop any of it."

Hunter looked at her.

"And that's why I'm going away. It's like the business with that watermelon seed. I don't want to do it and I can't stop any of it."

"But what about happiness?" Hunter said. "What about being happy?"

"Oh, Hunter. Happiness has nothing to do with anything."

.   .   .

The cold spell had broken and it was an unnaturally warm day in December when Rachel and Hunter stood on the front steps waiting for the cab that would take her to the station. She had insisted on the cab. "Less chance for drama," she said, and as with so many things lately, Hunter had seen the wisdom of that.

"You'll write?" he said.

"Of course I'll write."

"Write *me,* I mean."

They laughed then and she kissed him lightly on the cheek.

"I *do* love you, you know, Hunter. I do."

"Yes." And so he wouldn't cry, he said, "Do you see how good I'm being? No melodrama."

"It's only in art that you get melodrama," she said. "In life, endings are like this. See how easy?" But her voice shook as she spoke and there were tears on her face as she walked slowly to the cab that would take her away, for good.

6

The first time Rachel left him, Hunter used up all the normal dissipations and so this time he was forced to lose himself in work. Immediately after Christmas he went into the Chairman's office and volunteered to teach "Intro to Art: Medieval to Renaissance," which was a bitch of a lecture course that nobody ever wanted to teach. While the Chairman was still marveling at this unexpected show of collegiality, Hunter stunned him by saying he'd like to take on another course if one fell free. One *had* just fallen free, "Modern Art II: Realism and Impressionism," a showstopper so vastly overenrolled that the assigned lecturer had suffered a panic attack and, since he was rich anyhow, had bolted for Hawaii. Hunter offered to teach it. "How come?" the Chairman said, "What's going on?" and Hunter, without missing a beat, replied, "Instead of suicide." The Chairman thought for a minute, and then he nodded, saying, ambiguously, "Well, it's easier than studio work, isn't it."

· · ·

"It's all I bargained for," Rachel wrote from the convent guest house, "and that's not much. Still, I remain convinced that this is what I must do with my life."

Hunter stood in the foyer staring at her note for quite some time.

.   .   .

Everyone knew that Hunter had not been inside his studio in years. He no longer sculpted and he wouldn't talk about it and he wouldn't teach it. So when the rumor circulated that he would offer a studio workshop, there was curiosity and there was talk, some of which bore a faint resemblance to fact.

The official gossip went like this: the most famous sculptor of his generation, he had been blinded in a car crash and then miraculously restored to sight; either before or after the blinding, his wife left him; to retaliate, he slept with all the wives on campus and maybe a husband or two; finally, he had drunk himself nearly to death. And then, topping it all off, his wife returned to him just long enough to run away with his boyfriend.

When fall semester began, Hunter put up a little notice saying he would offer a studio tutorial for a few advanced graduate students. Nearly all the art majors applied. Hunter decided to accept three of them, but before he posted the names, a packet of photographs arrived, accompanied by a note saying, "I have no college degree, but I would like to study with you. Here are photos of my work." It was signed Joanne.

Hunter accepted the three graduate students and Joanne.

.   .   .

"Look at this, Joanne," he said. They were standing before her life-size sculpture of Hunter's head. "Look up at the head from underneath the chin. See? The interior construction has been badly built up here. That's why this cheekbone is set farther back than that one."

"I was rushing," she said. "I can fix that."

"It will always look fixed, though," he said. "Better to do the underwork right the first time."

"Got it," she said.

"And see this line above the eyes? It's soft. It's sentimental. And look at it in profile. See?"

"I see," she said.

"Do you know what's going on here? You're making a pitch for pity. Truly. Look at these lines. What they really ask for is that self-satisfied feeling people get when they see pain and don't feel it."

"Don't preach, Hunter, just tell me what's wrong."

"There's not much wrong," he said. "It's very good. It should be better, that's all."

"Oh Christ. So what am I supposed to do?"

"Try harder," he said.

When the sixteen weeks were done and Hunter said goodbye and wished them luck, he told Joanne he would work with her privately if she wanted. She said she'd have to think about it. She didn't have all that much ego left to spare.

He liked her style.

．　．　．

"Real art stirs us *up*," he said. Joanne had decided to work with him and Hunter was determined to pass on everything he knew. "Real art is disconcerting. It challenges us. It makes us *see*. Schlock, on the other hand, is easy to make and easy to look at, because its only job is to confirm easy impressions we already have about life and about ourselves. Think of a sit-com on television."

"I don't *want* to think of a sit-com on television, Hunter, I want to know how to give this thing its proper form."

He laughed. "You don't give things form, Joanne; you just cut away everything that conceals the form."

He liked her.

.   .   .

Rachel surprised him by sending a long letter about life in the convent as seen from the angle of the guest house. He had nearly forgotten what a hard cold eye she had and how deeply she could upset him.

"There is prayer and peace and love here," she wrote, "but there is pettiness and bickering and malice as well. God is here too, I suppose, but he's no more evident here in the convent than there in Boston. Still, this is where I am and where I have to be. Sometimes I wonder why."

Hunter sat down at once and composed a telegram that said, "Come back. Come back. Come back. I love you," and then he tore it up. If she were to come back, he knew, she'd have to be driven to it by God. If there was a God.

The next year there was no letter from her at all, not even a note.

.   .   .

Hunter and Joanne stood in silence before her figure of a dancer's torso. He suggested that she needed more space beneath the neck and shoulders and he explained how she could draw a wire around and through the neck and lift up the mass of the head without messing it all up.

She looked at the sculpture and thought for a long while.

"No, Hunter, I won't do that," Joanne said. "You may be right, and this piece might be better your way, but I see it this way, and this is how it's gonna be." She added, "Sorry."

They had been together two years now.

.   .   .

Joanne was a woman in her mid-forties, divorced, with three grown daughters. Middling attractive, she felt, and with lots

170

to offer. She considered who she was and who he was: his teaching, his prominence as a sculptor, the large body of his work. She considered, too, the cautionary tales about Rachel and Paul and even about poor Reba Cairn. And finally she thought to hell with it and said, "I realize, Hunter, that I'm only a minor character in all this, but I'd like to love you, if you'd care to let me."

Hunter laughed and said, "I need all the love I can get. I'm the original love pig." And he laughed again.

Nonetheless, he kept her at an emotional distance for a year, and then another. Only when he was convinced that she was it, the real thing, did he allow himself to love her in return. "What I want," he said, "before I die, is to *give* a little." He let it go at that.

Joanne knew what he meant: the love was greater on her side than on his.

. . .

Later—three years and three days later—when he lies dying in a subway in New York, Hunter will be thinking that he must call Joanne and tell her he is all right, even though he is not all right but in fact very close to death. His dying will take fifteen minutes. And he will think that this must be what Rachel meant about the randomness and waste of life, with no tidy resolutions and nothing to make it all cohere except, sometimes, a thin *thin* line of . . . what?

. . .

Rachel's yearly messages became more cryptic. "I don't like doing this, but I can, so I must. I ache with loneliness. I pray for strength. I send you love."

And the next year. "Forgive the self-indulgence of my note last year. It was a bad time. I discover, after all, that happiness has something to do with everything. I send you love, much love. I hope you are happy."

And the next. "His meddling in our lives, I think, is always for our good. Is that just sentimental? I send you love, dear Hunter, I send you all my love."

And the last was just a Christmas card signed, "Love, Rachel."

. . .

Joanne stood in the center of the studio marveling at what Hunter had made out of his life. She had unshrouded all the sculptures stored there and she spent the entire day moving from piece to piece, admiring, analyzing, passing judgment. She was puzzled by the Egyptian dog, Anubis, guardian of the dead. "It's just a copy," she said aloud to the empty room. "It's not even his." She moved on to other work, but she kept coming back to the Egyptian dog, which made her uncomfortable. It was all wrong. In some awful way, she knew it was bad luck. She threw the shroud around it once again and left the studio.

That night at dinner Joanne mentioned the dog to Hunter and asked him how it happened that he'd made a replica instead of something new. It seemed an odd thing for a sculptor to spend his time on. A lot of work. A lot of creative energy turned in upon itself. Hunter?

But Hunter was distracted, as he often was these days, and said, "We'll look at all of them. We'll go through the whole lot. As soon as I get back from New York."

7

Hunter went to New York to get a second opinion. He knew he was dying, but he went anyway because he owed it to Joanne and because it was the responsible thing to do. Now he just wanted to get back to Boston.

He was in Penn Station with a good three hours to kill. He checked his bag, and tried to think what to do next. He could walk, see a movie, waste some time at an art gallery. Blackie's gallery. Or he could sit here and look around him at the other, less expedient, forms of dying. For more than half his life he had been a sculptor and he knew true forms when he saw them.

As he went through the doors to Penn Plaza, he heard someone call, "Excuse me, sir?" He looked down and saw an old black man sitting on the floor. He had a green knitted ski cap on his head. One foot was bare and the other was wrapped in rags. He was holding his hand out to Hunter.

"Excuse me, sir," he said again. "Could I bother you for a hundred dollars."

Hunter laughed and the old black man laughed with him, a kind of recognition. They understood each other. In this one absurd exchange, they had cut through all the human layers of propriety and gunk and they had struck bedrock. Hunter gave him a dollar, and hung there, leaning over him, wanting to say something that would matter.

Almost at once a policeman came through the door and used his nightstick to prod the man, telling him to move on. The man shrugged and Hunter shrugged with him. "Sorry," the policeman said to Hunter. So much for bedrock.

Hunter walked slowly, going north and east, in the general direction of the Prescott Gallery. It was a good spring day in New York, with no breeze and just enough sun. For a minute or so Hunter was the only dying thing in sight. He should have opened his wallet and given that old black man everything he had, a free gift, corpse to corpse.

He kept on walking. After a while he came to Forty-fifth and Sixth, and in another minute he was standing before the A. H. Prescott Gallery. Austin Harrold Prescott III. Small wonder he called himself Blackie.

It was ten years or more since the Great Mistake—"the physical union of our two spirits," as Blackie called it—that night when Hunter, drunk and reckless, took him to bed just for the hell of it and brought upon himself ten years of well-deserved guilt. Since then, they had seen each other only twice and both times Hunter had paid heavy interest on that guilt. It was now just over a year since he had seen Blackie.

He paused outside the gallery and looked in. Somebody named Brit Botchkis was on display. What he could see through the window looked like dogshit, painted in pastels and mounted on chrome pedestals.

He pushed open the heavy door and at once he was enveloped by that voice and that presence. "Hunter! Dear Hunter! What a delight to see you! I mean I'm overwhelmed! And how well you look! Well, my dear man, you do!" It was Austin Prescott, tall, sepulchrally thin, and with a mass of dyed black hair.

Hunter shook his hand and smiled. "Blackie," he said, and was surprised at the trembling in his voice.

They looked at each other.

"Well, it's been years! I mean absolutely! Let me just look at you!" Blackie lowered his voice confidentially. "How have you been keeping, Hunter?"

"Dying," Hunter said, "but otherwise pretty well."

"Such a one!" Blackie said, and led Hunter past the dogshit to his office at the back of the gallery.

For the next half hour Blackie talked, excited, about the horrors of the new painting, the new sculpture, the new way everything was coming apart. Not just the art world, but all of civilization: there was AIDS, and muggings, and that crew in Washington, and just yesterday a perfectly dreadful woman in the apartment next door had been strangled to death by a Gristede's delivery boy. Gristede's! "Reason is captiv'd," Blackie said. "My dear, the center cannot hold."

Hunter listened and Blackie talked, in a frenzy to entertain.

Hunter smiled. He nodded. After a while this installment on the debt was nearly paid. "My train," he said.

"Oh, but you mustn't, you simply cannot dash away now, dear Hunter, because it's obvious that fate has brought you here! I mean it's perfect! Isn't it absolutely perfect? Because now I can consult with you about you know *who!* Do you know?"

Paul Bates, of course. The Prescott had been showing Bates up until last week.

"Can you guess?"

Hunter shook his head no.

"Paul Bates."

"Oh?"

"You were very close once. Or so I hear. Not that he told me anything, mind you, Hunter. He thinks you're some kind of god."

"He was a student of mine."

"I know that. Simply everybody knows *that.*" Blackie paused. "But there was nothing between you? I mean he just wasn't . . .?"

"Nothing," Hunter said. "He wasn't. I'm not. There was nothing."

"Except for that once. *Avec moi.*"

"Except for that once. For which I apologize. It was cruel and stupid and . . . and I apologize."

"Poor Paul Bates," Blackie said. "I thought there might be *some*thing to explain the way he's been. You do know, don't you, that he's spent years, I mean simply years and years, working on that Abraham and Isaac. Oh yes! Truly! He hacked away at the one you helped him with until it looked like a pile of *stones,* Hunter. I mean it was *très* pitiful. And then he tried to do another one and then another one, and I kept advancing him money all the time, and finally I said

to him, 'My dear,' I said, 'you've simply got to put that al-
batross away. It's Hunter's, anyway, so forget about it and
just do something.' And finally he just did."

"I never helped with an Abraham and Isaac."

"Well, I know. But perhaps you should have. Well, what
he's doing now has sold very very well, I mean he's *très riche*
after just this one show, but frankly it's the same old stuff
he did before except the life's gone out of it. It's too sad,
Hunter. It just truly is."

"Yes, it's sad."

"But this is where you come in. You have the chance
to make him rich and famous! Today! I cast the deciding
vote, and if you absolutely insist, I'll vote for him, and he'll
get tax-free thousands—sixty of them—every year until
eternity."

"Sixty? They've gone up?"

"It's a *Living* Grant. The cost of living has gone up."

Hunter knew these grants. They were intended to allow
artists to work and just forget about earning money, but in
fact they always went to whoever was hot. And whoever was
hot already had money, or access to it. Even if, to get it, they
had to churn out copies of old work, gone dead. It killed him
that Paul would stoop to something like that. It took his
breath away.

"Well, what do you think, Hunter? The other big con-
tender is Brit Botchkis." He pointed to the gallery out front.
"She's very big right now."

"Give it to her."

"Not Bates?"

"Botchkis."

"Well, as Norman says, 'Life is a bitch.' "

Hunter slumped a little in his chair and Blackie stared at
him, frowning. In a new voice, deeper, with no affectation,
he asked, "Are you all right, Hunter?"

Hunter had gone gray. He started to get up and then sat down again, out of breath. Blackie leaned toward him, studying the taut skin of the face, the black smudges beneath the eyes, the aura of death. "Cancer?" he asked. Hunter sat with his eyes closed.

"How long have you got?" Blackie asked.

"Three months."

"I've got six."

"So I'll get there first." This was the moment when he should reach out and grip Blackie's hand, give him the comfort of a friend's embrace. Blackie knew it too and sat forward, ready.

Hunter waited until the moment passed. Then he smiled again and walked out of the office and through the gallery, not looking at the dogshit done in pink and fawn and violet, mounted on chrome.

Blackie followed him, and at the door he made one last stand: "Why not give it to Bates then?"

Hunter looked at him.

"Bates," Blackie said. "For the grant."

Hunter waved the question aside. "Take heart, Blackie," he said. "Take care."

.   .   .

As he was sitting there talking to Blackie, a pain had struck him squarely in the chest and for a second he'd thought that this was it, that he had literally run out of breath. But the pain passed as quickly as it had come, leaving him with this dazed feeling, as if some part of his brain had fallen under a shadow.

Out on the street, the sun was still shining but a wind had come up. There would be a storm later. He could tell. He crossed the street and walked north for a block, discovered his error, and looked around, uncertain. He was not lost; he was just upset about Paul and Blackie and, to tell the truth, about himself. He got his bearings then. He would cross the street, walk south, and . . .

Suddenly a woman screamed. There was a terrible squeal of rubber, the sound of metal crashing against metal, a hoarse yell. Hunter had crossed against the light, and a taxi, brakes screeching, plowed into the car ahead. People gathered, shouting; an argument broke out. A pretzel man on the sidewalk grabbed Hunter by the arm and yelled at him, "Chrissake, do you want to kill yourself!"

Hunter pulled away and kept on walking, blindly. He did not want to kill himself. He had too much wrong to put right before he could think of killing himself. Besides, cancer was doing that for him. It was slowly, purposefully chipping away the rock until the shape of things could be revealed.

. . . .

Somehow he reached Penn Station. People were rushing through the doors, past him, toward him, and Hunter stopped at the head of the stairs to get his breath. He was dizzy still. He had to think.

"Move it, Pops," somebody said and pushed him gently to one side. He found himself looking down at an old derelict, one foot bare, the other wrapped in rags. He was a black man with a green knitted ski cap pulled down almost to his eyes. He had his hand out.

Hunter recognized him and immediately lost his sense of confusion. "Yes," he said, "of course," and pulled out his wallet. He pressed a five-dollar bill into the man's hand, thinking, I should give him ten. No, a hundred. He began ticking through his twenties when somebody jostled him hard from behind and the wallet flew from his hands.

The black man scrambled across the floor and retrieved it. He sat back and turned the wallet over in his hands, smoothing the soft leather, and then he flipped it open. He fanned his thumb over the thick packet of bills. After a long time he held the wallet up to Hunter, almost but not quite within his reach. A funny smile played at his mouth.

He stared at Hunter and Hunter stared back.

Hunter's vision was very clear at this moment and he saw not an old black derelict but a man worth sculpting. He was not old, after all. Nor was he black. He was a sooty color, with a wide brow and deep black eyes. His thick aquiline nose nearly touched the scraggly hairs of his upper lip. His mouth was thin and hard, even now when he was smiling, and he had a long pointed chin. Anyone modeling that face in clay would have to press very hard with the thumbs to achieve the depth of those eyes, and it would take a kind of genius to catch the hatred they held. You could never do it in mere stone. He had a face like a rattlesnake, the hard dusty skin, the glittering eyes.

They continued to assess each other, the man smiling, Hunter making calculations.

"No reward?" the man said. His smile faded and was replaced by a look of sardonic amusement.

Hunter reached the extra distance and took the wallet from the man's extended hand. He pulled out another five. "Here," he said. "Now we're quits."

"No, we're not," he said and continued to stare at Hunter, making the look into some kind of threat.

.   .   .

Downstairs in the waiting room Hunter discovered he still had an hour before train time. He felt filthy. He wanted to wash and he probably should pee, but he hated public restrooms, so he decided he would just put up with feeling dirty and uncomfortable.

He browsed in the bookstalls until he found himself among the racks of Harlequin Romances, Gothics, Camfields, Annendales, and finally a whole string of Victoria Heaths. But to his surprise, there were only two new ones, *Love's Deceit* and *Love Fulfilled*. Did this mean that Rachel had stopped writing her Flambeau novels? She'd found love at last? He bought them both and sat down to read.

But he couldn't concentrate. The awful prose stopped him dead and all he could think of was the patience and care and love that she and Paul had lavished on him when he was blind. He wanted forgiveness. He wanted to make up for everything. For something. For anything.

He went to a telephone and called the Prescott Gallery. A woman answered. Mr. Prescott, she said, had left for the day. No, she could not give out his home number but, yes, she would take a message.

"The message is simply: give the grant to Bates. And sign it: Love, Hunter. Do you have that?"

The woman sniffed; she did not approve. "Give the grant to Bates," she said. "I have that."

"And it's signed: Love, Hunter."

"Yes," she said, and hung the phone up just a little too firmly. In spite of himself, Hunter laughed out loud.

• • •

He found an empty bench near the checkroom and sat down to wait. Almost at once a gang of kids came charging in and took over the rest of the bench. They slung their duffel bags on the floor around them. The girls fell into noisy personal conversations about what Jennifer had said to Jeffrey and whether that meant they were broken up or not. The boys hung together, silent. Hunter glanced over at them. All the girls were smoking; one of the boys was drinking from a flask. They were rich kids from Westport and Greenwich and Fairfield. Fourteen or fifteen years old, with clean skin and expensively shabby clothes.

Suddenly in their midst appeared a crazy lady. She was dressed well enough in a tan skirt and white blouse, a tan bag, tan shoes, but the giveaway was her white ankle socks. Years ago Hunter had formulated, for Rachel's amusement, what he called Hunter's Law: any woman who wears white ankle socks in public is certifiably insane. He had never seen an exception to the rule.

"What lovely hair," she said to one of the girls. "Now what's your name and where are you from? Come on, tell me." The girl giggled and looked to her friends for support. They giggled too. "Now don't make fun of an older person. That's rude, do you hear? Didn't your parents teach you better than that? I'm sure they did. Come on, we'll start again. Let's be friendly now." Her voice was bright, and Hunter could hear in it the craziness and despair. "What's your name and where are you from?"

Hunter knew how it would go. The kids would put up with her as long as they could, and then somebody would say something funny, and somebody else would say something rude, and then they'd freeze her out with laughter and silence, and finally the crazy lady would go away. The kids would laugh and talk about it and laugh some more, and then be sick with shame when they got home that night.

It was horrible, all of it. The waste and the cruelty. Nothing made sense. Nothing was connected to anything else. Blackie was right, reason is captiv'd indeed.

Hunter closed his eyes and pretended sleep. At once the face of the fake black man flew up before him. The man's eyes were on fire with rage. Against his will, Hunter studied the man's eyes until they flickered and went out.

At the other end of the bench the crazy lady was saying, "Now, come on now. You can't be rude to older people. Let's be friendly. Tell me your name." She was answered by hard laughter and a muttered comment from one of the boys.

He got up. He could bear it no longer and besides he was desperate to pee.

He went downstairs to the men's room and was struck by the rancid smell even before he reached the door. Inside, the floor was covered in a thick slick of water and dirt, and the stench was terrible. Nobody was there. Hunter stood in the puddled floor and peed into the filthy urinal. He tried to make his mind a blank. He finished, and turned to one of the sinks to wash his hands.

A stall door opened and a skinny boy, twelve or thirteen, came out and stood in front of him. "Can I have some money?" he said.

Hunter washed his hands and shook them dry. He looked at the small boy and saw jail in his face.

"Why?" Hunter said. "Explain to me exactly why I should give you money."

"Because you've got plenty and I don't have none."

"Very good," Hunter said. Truth was rare and the least you could give it was money. He laughed and reached for his wallet.

In the silence, three other boys emerged from the stalls and formed a semicircle around the first one. They stood facing Hunter. A fourth boy, much older, wearing heavy boots and a leather bracelet with studs, came out of another stall and walked around behind Hunter.

So here it is.

And then, as if he had shouted for help, the men's room door opened and a policeman came in. The young boys scat-tered to the stalls, but the older one stepped up to the urinal and unzipped his pants. Slowly, staring at the policeman the whole time, he took out his heavy penis and cradled it in his palm as if he were weighing it. The policeman stared back. "Everything all right here?" he said, turning from the boy at the urinal to Hunter. "You all right?" Hunter nodded, speechless, and left the men's room.

At the top of the stairs someone grabbed his arm. It was the crazy lady with the white ankle socks. Hunter pulled away.

"Oh no you don't," she said. "You thought you were going to get out of it, didn't you? Now, let's be friendly. Come on. Don't make fun of an older person. Now tell me. What's your name and where are you from? Hmmmm?"

.   .   .

It was twenty minutes to train time and the gate had just been posted. Number 18. That was down at the far end of the station near the stairs to the men's room. Near the murderous boys.

Hunter retrieved his suitcase from Baggage Check and made his way to the benches nearest Gate 18. He sat down and closed his eyes. Suddenly he felt a fiery pain behind them, like a hot needle driven deep into his brain. He was going to die, and he had made sense of nothing. It was all chaos and waste and good people doing bad things. If only, like Rachel, he could find some thread that pulled it all together.

He opened his eyes. He was looking into a large open hand. A huge black man stood before him, stooped, dressed in layers of rags. "Can you help me?" he was saying, and he moved his hand closer to Hunter's chest.

Hunter was dizzy from his thoughts and from the pain. He looked around the waiting area and found that everyone was staring at him. There was absolute silence. All the faces were black and all of them were hostile. To him.

"Can you help me?" the man said again.

Hunter looked up at the man, his purpled skin, his sunken eyes. Of course he would help him. But he made no move toward his wallet. He looked at the hostile people staring at him, waiting to see what he would do. He saw in their stares a picture of himself beaten and bloody on the waiting room floor, as they kicked his face, his belly, his unprotected spine. Why? What had he done to them?

Despite his terror, he looked coldly at the man before him, shook his head no, and lowered his eyes as if he were going to take a nap. He could see the hand still thrust toward him.

Through the silence came an angry voice. "Don't ask him for money. Take it."

The hand was still outstretched.

"Take it. Whitey's taken it from us all our lives. Take it from him. It's yours anyway. By rights."

The silence went on.

"Take that fucking wallet out of his pocket and kick the shit out of him, man! Do it!"

Suddenly the hand was yanked away and the other man, the furious one, stood before him. He thrust his fist in Hunter's face.

"Give him your fucking money, fool. All of it."

No one moved, no one called out. Hunter was on his own. He stared at the fist and then up at the man who was threatening him. He was short but heavily muscled, with gold chains around his neck, and he wore a red tee shirt with BROTHER printed on it in black.

Hunter shook his head no.

The man grabbed Hunter's shirtfront with one hand and began slowly to twist it in a tight knot. Suddenly another hand, soot-colored and powerful, clamped hard on the man's wrist, forcing him to release his grip on Hunter.

"We can discuss this, brother. No need to upset this gen'man."

He wore a green knitted ski cap and his feet were now firmly planted in army boots. It was the fake black man from upstairs.

He relaxed his grasp on the black man's wrist, stared him

down, and after a moment he pointed to the BROTHER on the man's chest and then to the gold chains about his neck. "Very nice, brother," he said softly. "Very very nice."

"Now," he said, turning to Hunter. "You seem to need some assistance. I *know* what you've got in that wallet. Why don't you just hand that over to me and I'll guarantee you get on that train with your ticket and your credit cards and all the nice pictures of your loved ones, and I'll see to it that brother here doesn't upset you any longer. Isn't that right, brother?"

The two men faced off. In a trance, Hunter reached for his wallet, and held it out to the fake black man. Of course there would be no policeman this time. Of course no one would do anything to stop what must happen. And then it happened.

Brother lunged at the wallet. At the same moment the fake black man reached for his switchblade. But the knife failed him this time, and during that second when the blade lodged useless in the handle, Brother pulled out his own knife and thrust it in and up, deep into the man's belly. The wallet fell from Hunter's hand and the fake black man collapsed on top of it.

There were gasps, a snicker, someone said, "No, oh no," but nobody called for help, and in a moment everybody had disappeared from the area except Hunter. He sat there, dumb, looking at the bleeding man. And then Hunter too got up and left. He did not know why, but he knew—as if he had been through it in a dream—that this is what came next.

Gate 18 was still locked and so Hunter moved on to 16 and then 14 and then 12. The door gave. Hunter opened it and descended the stairs to the platform below. He looked far down both ends of the platform. He was alone. He turned to the right and walked slowly, as far as he could, to the end.

Darkness. Echoes. He could hear his hard pulse. He stopped and waited, his back pressed against the blackened wall.

For a long time there was only silence. Then he heard what he was waiting for: the sound of the door being opened, feet on the stairs, purposeful and slow. It was either a very old person or someone in great pain.

The footsteps were coming along the platform in his direction. Hunter looked up and saw that it was, of course, the fake black man. He moved in a shuffling walk, barely able to lift his feet. As the man approached, Hunter could see his left hand pressed against his stomach to staunch the flow of blood. In his right he clutched an open knife.

Hunter did not move. The man stood before him, blood oozing from his wound and covering his left hand, and he tried to gather his breath. He looked at the blood dripping to the floor and then he looked into Hunter's face. Hunter looked back.

He had expected the face of pure evil, but it was only an ordinary face, wedge-shaped, with deep glittering eyes. The eyes were clouded now, tired, giving the man the determined look of someone doing the thing he must. He could have been a sculptor finishing a difficult piece of work.

He plunged the knife into Hunter's chest just below the collarbone. He pulled it out and struck again, this time higher. He struck again, but the knife glanced against Hunter's ribs.

"Why?" Hunter whispered. "We don't even know each other."

The man struck again; this time he inserted the knife carefully in Hunter's sternum but the knife did not go fully in. He sighed, and slumped against Hunter's chest. They stood there, pressed against each other at the black wall.

"Why?" Hunter said. A small stream of blood trickled from his mouth onto the man's shoulder.

The man tipped his head back for a moment, and slowly,

purposefully, he leaned into Hunter and licked the blood from his lower lip. He slid to the ground and lay there motionless.

Hunter remained upright, his hand to his mouth—hanging on as long as he must, trying to understand—and then he collapsed onto the dirty floor.

He was losing consciousness. His mind was muddled. But he could not go yet. He had to call Joanne to say he was all right. And Rachel; he should call her. And Paul and Blackie and that crazy Reba Cairn and Lon Chi and that girl in class and then—the artist's luck—he saw what Rachel meant. It was all meaningless chaos except for that thin thin line. And then he died.

When they found the bodies, the face of the murderer was without expression. Hunter's face, though, perhaps because of those old scars near his mouth, seemed to have a smile, as if he might yet wake and live.

IV: MARÍA LUZ BUENVIDA

I will tell you the worst right away, and then after that you can see how all this has come about. You will not have to worry that there is something unspeakable to follow. I am telling you the unspeakable now.

The soldiers have raped me and cut off my breasts and slit my throat. They have done other things with a knife: one of them made a star shape down there around my sex, another one carved the shape of a cross on my face. They have left me for dead, these four soldiers of the Military Police. And of course I will be dead, in minutes.

So that is the worst. Now you have nothing else to fear.

My name is María Luz Buenvida. I am the daughter of Jorge Buenvida, the filmmaker, and of Helena Curtin, who is American. My brother, Miguel, is one year older than me, and I am eighteen. That is my family. Like me, they are all dead or dying.

Until a year ago we were very wealthy; we were one of the privileged families of our country. We had a large apartment in the city and, though we almost never went there, we also had a ranch in the hills. I attended the convent school taught by the French nuns and Miguel was enrolled in the university. My father made films. My mother supervised the housekeeper and the parties and played with Mimi, her miniature poodle. We were very happy; and we were safe, we thought.

You must understand that we did not live like most people in the capital. My father's films meant that he had all kinds of friends and business acquaintances: actors, painters, poets, screenwriters, shipping people, even high officers in the army. Most of his friends, of course, were from our own country, but he had others who were American, Greek, French, Italian, and he spoke their languages. Mostly we spoke English at home, at first because my mother was uncomfortable speaking Spanish and later because all my father's friends seemed to prefer it. English was chic. At parties—and we had large parties in those days, almost every weekend—there would be a lot of drinking and a lot of loud conversation and everyone would be speaking English with a different accent, calling my father George and my brother Mikey, Americanizing every name. It was at one such party, I suppose, that it all began.

"Your father's films. Do you understand them?" It was Colonel García, old and fat and a little drunk; he was flanked, as always, by two soldiers of the Guardia, the Military Police. He spoke to me in Spanish. "Do you?"

"I like them," I said.

"Spanish, please," he said, and so I repeated "I like them," in Spanish.

"Are you ashamed to speak Spanish?" he asked, smiling. "Is it because of your American mother?"

Guests, even military guests, do not talk this way to their hosts unless they have a reason. Behind his smile there was some kind of threat; though the Buenvida money and prestige has always kept us outside the reach of the military, I was careful how I answered.

"Colonel," I said, "you misunderstand. I am proud to speak Spanish. In fact, my English and my French are very weak. It is just that film people, sometimes, like to speak English."

"Your father's films. I do not understand them."

"He is a poet, my father."

"They are never contemporary; always they are set in some time long past. Why is that, do you suppose? A man like your father is a man of our times, not of yesterday. And yet, he is not a political man, your father. Is he?"

"No," I said. "Not political."

"Sometimes . . ." He stood silently, examining the olive in his glass; after a moment he picked up the olive between his thumb and his forefinger, held it toward me, and—with no trace of any emotion—he squeezed the pimento from the heart of the olive into my glass. ". . . Sometimes, one must be."

Later that night, of course, I told my father everything that had happened, everything except what Colonel García had done with the olive.

"García's a drunk," my father said. "He can't touch us." He thought for a while. "No," he said, "he has no power over us. Just forget about him. And don't mention this to your mother."

Naturally I would not have mentioned it to my mother.

She was a woman who lived in constant terror: of sickness, of revolution, of investigation. And so she drank. But as an American, she was quite safe. We were all quite safe.

In a week or two, I forgot about Colonel García, or at least I succeeded in putting him out of my conscious mind. My father had completed his new film, *Ifigenia,* and was busy editing it. Our long school holiday had begun and so I was able to go with him, sit in the editing room, and watch how he worked. He liked having me with him. During those weeks I learned—though I did not understand until much later; indeed, until now—what a good filmmaker my father was, and what a great man.

It is true, as García said, that my father has never made a contemporary film. He cannot. He cannot indict the military and the aristocracy and, yes, the clergy except under the cloak of ancient history. And to that history, which he cannot alter, he brings his own mystical belief: that from all this suffering there must eventually come some kind of redemption. And so his films seem to be mythological, even fantastic, to some critics. But always they are a metaphor for our lives today. My father was very much a political man.

. . .

We gave no parties during these weeks and my father, who spent all day at the studio and all evening planning the next day's work, made it clear he wanted Miguel and me out of the house in the evening. He said it was not good for young people to mope about as we did, that we ought to be with people our own age, that we ought to get out and have fun.

"Le Disco," Miguel said. "That's where I always go."

Actually, my father did not want us to see my mother pour herself a new drink each hour, growing calm around ten o'clock, and at midnight resigned—for the next few hours—to her life in exile. That is how she thought of her life here, as exile. Because even if she had been brave enough to return to the States, she had nobody to return to. Her parents were dead. No brothers or sisters. She had only us. And she was drifting away from us much faster than my father knew. She did not understand that Miguel and I are of this country, that we love it, that we do not want to run away. By this time she had given up trying to convince me to go to college in the States; she had long since given up on Miguel; she clung only to Mimi, her little white poodle, who sat in her lap and slept on her bed and, no matter what the occasion, was never allowed out of her sight.

And so, to please my father, Miguel and I went dancing at Le Disco. I hated it. The boys in their tight jeans and their hundred-dollar silk shirts. The girls waiting, teasing. Everyone desperately having fun, dancing and shrieking so as not to think of what lay out there in the darkened streets: the National Police, the Army Police, the Treasury Police, the Secret Police, the Guardia, the steel-plated Toyotas circling the block, the small black cars driven by men who concealed their faces beneath military caps and sunglasses, all the trappings of terror. And inside, the noise and the light. Strobe lights in all the colors of blood. Metal clashing on metal. The smell of perfume and sweat. Only the occasional disfigurement warned of the world outside Le Disco. A slashed ear, a long scar on one side of the nose, the whitened burn mark from cheek to chin: these were the victims of interrogation, dangerous to be seen with, untouchables.

It was my fault that one of these, Virgilio Bellorin, a photographer for *La prensa,* was put through a second interrogation. Miguel was dancing with some girl from the university and I was standing against a wall, thinking of my mother and how she was moving deeper into drink. I found myself staring, without realizing it, at a young man who looked almost exactly like Miguel. He had the same thin face and the same anxious eyes, but wore his hair long, almost to his shoulders. This gave him a soft look, almost feminine, and it struck me suddenly that he looked more like me than like Miguel. And because at that moment the gods who manipulate our lives willed that he come over and stand next to me, I turned to him and said, "We could be twins."

He smiled at me, his lips parting slowly over his perfect white teeth, and he said, "Well, I would like that." There has never been a smile more beautiful.

And so I fell in love with him, at that moment, forever, and with only nine words spoken between us.

He was looking at me, and I returned his look, but I could think of nothing to say. I had been so forward. I was confused. And he said nothing.

But then he pushed back his hair from his left cheek, exposing a long thick scar, and said simply, "But there is this."

Before I could realize what he was telling me, he turned abruptly and left. At once Miguel appeared at my side, and said, "Are you crazy? Have you lost your mind? We've got to get out of here," and took my arm and rushed me to the door. "Guardia," he said, indicating with a jerk of his head the Military Police standing by the entrance. "They may have seen you." And of course they had.

We came out the door of Le Disco just as two of the Guardia were pushing Virgilio into a small black Datsun; they climbed into the car and the car roared away before they had even closed the doors. But by this time two others had taken me by the arms and lifted me from the stairs. I heard Miguel shouting and someone pushed from behind and one of the soldiers let me go. I tried to break free and run, but the other soldier pushed me hard against the car, my hands behind my back. I could see nothing, but I heard cursing and the sound of fists against flesh. Someone groaned in pain, a body hit the pavement, people were running. And then my head was pounded hard against the car door and when I woke I was in a tiny interrogation room.

Someone was asking me over and over how long I had known Virgilio Bellorin, what was my relationship with him, did I know he was a subversive.

"My name is Buenvida," I said finally. "I am the daughter of Jorge Buenvida, the filmmaker. And of Helena Curtin, who is an American citizen."

"We know quite well who you are, señorita. We have been through your purse and all your cards of identity. But things are not now for you and your family what they once were. Do you understand that? You are now just another suspect being interviewed. Please notice, interviewed; not interrogated. Now let us try again. How long have you known Virgilio Bellorin?" No one touched me. No one interrogated me.

After an hour or more they let me go. My father was in the waiting room, furious but strangely quiet. He had asked to see Colonel García but was told the colonel could not be disturbed except on important matters. He had made demands, issued threats, promised reprisal, but he had gotten nowhere. He had decided then to get me free first of all, and only afterward get revenge.

"You see, señor?" the soldier said, as he led me into the room. "Here is your daughter, safe and sound. Our little interview is finished."

"I walked slowly to my father's side. There was no embrace. "Miguel?" I whispered. My father nodded.

"And you, señor? You are calmer now. That is good. Because things have changed for you here. As you see."

Things had changed more than we knew. A realignment in the government, a shift in military power, a payoff, a betrayal, a murder: who could guess what really had happened? But Colonel García was now a powerful man and he was convinced that my father was a threat to him.

. . .

A long time passed, a month, two months, and nothing happened to us. My father was finishing the editing of *Ifigenia* with the meticulous care he brought to all his films, frame by frame, image by image, and I sat next to him the whole time, learning how to conspire for freedom.

Miguel had survived his fight with the Guardia with only a broken rib and a great number of bruises. It was he who insisted that we go back now and then to Le Disco and it was there that I again saw, but did not speak to, Virgilio Bellorin. "Don't!" Miguel said as I moved, appalled, toward Virgilio, and later on the dance floor Miguel said, "Don't you see I am one of them?" Le Disco was where they set up their meetings and passed on messages. But I could not think what it meant that my brother was a revolutionary; I could think only of Virgilio's face, his mouth scarred, his beautiful smile shattered. It seemed to me at that moment that our country's freedom came at too high a cost.

Our family's freedom ended the following day. I was sitting on one side of my father, his assistant on the other, as we watched him study the movement of Ifigenia's hand in a series of ten frames. The gesture must appear to be ultimate resignation, he said, and everything depended on the length of time the gesture took. Fewer frames or more?

"Notice the difference it makes," he said, but he never finished his sentence, because at that moment the door burst open and the room filled with Military Police, rifles cocked and pointed, and someone said softly, almost sweetly, "You are under arrest." In no more than a minute my father was handcuffed and taken away, and in a few minutes more they had gathered every reel of film in the room and taken that away too. A single soldier remained. I was crouched in a corner, my hands at my face, and this soldier came to me and helped me to my feet. And then lightly, as if it were an accident, he touched me between my legs and said, "Perhaps you will be next." He smiled at me, and left.

Miguel and I spent the rest of the day at the prison trying to get some information about Father. They would tell us nothing. We asked to see Colonel García but we were told the colonel could not be disturbed except on important matters. Go home and wait, they told us, and finally, at six o'clock, they turned us out.

We had decided not to tell Mother, but when we got home, she already knew. "What has happened to your father?" she said. "They've taken him, haven't they? They've arrested him." And then she told us about the telephone call. Military Police had seized our ranch in the hills, confiscated the cattle and all movables, and burnt the buildings to the ground. They claimed that the ranch was a safe house for revolutionaries. No charge had yet been brought, nor had anyone official contacted her; the telephone call was anonymous, from a friend.

We lit candles at the cathedral that night, and prayed, and then we sat in the living room in silence, Bach and then Telemann playing in the background, until at last we could say it was time to go to bed. My mother had nothing to drink.

The next morning, early, Miguel went to keep vigil at the police station; my mother and I went to the American embassy. The former ambassador and his wife had been to our parties often, had even requested private screenings of my father's films, but several months ago a new ambassador had been appointed. We did not know him. He was more aloof than his predecessor, spent more time within his compound than outside it, and had turned the embassy itself into a fortress. He represented, so *La prensa* said, the increased hostility of the new American administration.

My mother and I were admitted to the embassy and were told we would have to wait. An armed guard took us to a small sitting room and left us there, and after an hour or so an old woman in a maid's uniform brought us coffee. My mother asked her when someone would finally see us, but the woman only shook her head and said nothing. My mother paced the room, her hands trembling. I sat and thought of my father, and of Miguel, and of Virgilio. How had any of this happened? And why? After another hour, my mother was asked to step into the next room. There she was allowed to tell her story to a secretary, and afterward to an assistant, and after that to another assistant, who took notes. I waited, my hands knotted in my lap, sure we were being betrayed. At the end the American ambassador himself spoke with her, listened, and then rose to dismiss her. "We will do whatever we can," he said. "It is not easy."

At home, my mother took Mimi from the arms of the housekeeper and clutched the little dog to her breast. "I'll never see Jorge again," she said. "They'll murder him. We'll all be murdered in this terrible place." But again, she did not drink.

Miguel had news, and not good news. My father was accused of crimes against the republic: giving arms and a safe house to revolutionaries, financing the vigilante movement, seeking to overthrow the legitimate government. These charges were not yet public; it was not clear they would even bother with charges at this point; there was plenty of time, now. Colonel García himself had passed on this news to Miguel, taking care to add that the principal charge against my father was his revolutionary propaganda—namely, the film

Ifigenia. "Tell your sister," he said, "that I understand your father's films quite well now."

And so we concluded that my father must still be alive. Imprisoned, certainly. Tortured, we had no doubt. But still alive, and still able someday to return home. Others had returned. He might. And so, for the moment, we had hope.

. . . .

Despite our hope, or to sustain it, we took the precaution of going each day to the cathedral, evidently to light a candle for Father, but actually so that we could pass through the cathedral cloister to the archbishop's palace where, in a waiting room, out of the scrutiny of the police, we examined the photos of the disappeared.

Virgilio, Miguel told me, was one of the photographers responsible for these photos. Every day he risked his life taking these photographs and doubled the risk by getting them seen. Some he was able to place in *La prensa* as news items. "Woman and two daughters killed; assailants unknown. Bodies of three men discovered in a suburban *barraca;* headless, castrated; assailants unknown. Two nuns raped and murdered; bodies discovered in an alley; assailants unknown." Some of these photos were printed on broadsides and, under cover of night, hung up in shopping malls, in movie theaters, in streetcars. But the archbishop's palace was the main clearinghouse for these photographs.

The five heavy picture albums were bound in white plastic, their covers decorated with pastel scenes from American cigarette advertisements: a young woman in a filmy dress, a handsome man, a stream, a weeping willow tree. And inside were pictures of missing people, the disappeared. The whole world has seen newspaper photographs of the body dumps at El Playón, but in our country—officially—El Playón does not exist. Nonetheless Virgilio and others have photographed

the dead, the evidence of torture and mutilation still fresh
on their bodies. Cigarette burns on the breasts of young girls.
Hands and feet lopped off with blunt knives. A severed head,
its eyes gouged out. And, always, young men who have been
castrated, their genitals stuffed in their mouths.

Miguel and I sat together, turning page after page of the
most recent photographs. When we finished, sick, nearly
dumb, I asked Miguel, "Did Father know this?" Miguel nodded. "This is what all his films are about," he said.

Things went on in this way for some time. Each day my
mother would put Mimi into the arms of the housekeeper
and then go to the American embassy and ask for help. Miguel
and I would check the newest photographs and afterward,
still hoping, we would go to the nearest police station and
ask to see my father. At night the three of us would have
dinner together, pretend to listen to music, and then go to
bed. During this time we knew, of course, that our house
was watched, and that we were followed in the street. A long
black car with smoked glass windows was stationed day and
night across the street from our apartment building; one man
in front, two in back, ready. Nonetheless at least once a week
Miguel would slip out in the middle of the night to rendez-
vous with the Student Liberation Front. He gave me a number
I could telephone, a code I could use to identify myself and
to ask about him, just in case some morning he did not return
at dawn. He would not give me the code for Virgilio.

Then one morning Miguel did not come home. I told my
mother he was sleeping late, he had a headache, he was worn
out, and so she left for the embassy suspecting nothing. Every
second hour that day I called the number Miguel had given
me and I used the code: I was a Marx Brothers fan and could
someone tell me at what time *A Night at the Opera* was playing. "Wrong number," a man said, and hung up. If there were
news, he would have called back immediately. No one called.

That night, with no Miguel, with no telephone call from an anonymous friend, I had to tell Mother he was missing.

At first she was very calm. "This is the end," she said, and rocked Mimi in her arms. "This is how it all ends." But after a while she began to sob, and she did not stop. I tried to comfort her, I brought her a glass of water, but her sobbing became wild, she began to scratch her face, and claw at her hair. She was hysterical. I stood there, helpless, useless, and then I thought of my father and my brother, and I slapped her, hard. After a moment I got her a cold cloth for her face. "Try to remember who you are," I said to her. She lay down in her bedroom then; she did not want dinner. She wanted nothing, she said, except to forget. At midnight, hearing her at the liquor cabinet, I got up, put on my robe, and went out to her. "Please," I said. "Not now." She looked at me as if she hated me, and then she poured herself another tumbler of brandy. "Mother," I said, but it was too late.

Virgilio Bellorin came to my bed that night. He was suddenly there at the door to my room; I had not heard a sound; I was not afraid.

"Miguel is all right," he said. "there was shooting. Two police were killed. The Guardia didn't get him, but he may have been recognized."

I wanted to ask, where is he? And where is my father? And how did you get in here? And what is happening to all of us? Instead I asked only, "*Is* he all right?"

"You should know nothing. If you are interrogated, it is better that you know nothing. He is all right."

"Sit here," I said, touching the side of the bed. I put a finger on the left side of his mouth. "They have hurt you," I said. "You have a scar." I traced his lips with my finger, and he licked my finger with his tongue, and I raised my head to kiss him on the mouth. He kissed me back and then pulled away.

"Not from pity," he said.

"From love," I said.

And so we made love until nearly dawn and during that time I forgot my father and my mother and my brother. I gave myself up to myself.

.   .   .

The next morning, my mother was awake before I was. Sick from drink but desperate and determined, she announced she was going to accompany me to the police station and she was going to make demands. One last attempt, she said.

"Miguel is safe," I said, but when she asked me how I knew, I only shrugged and said I just felt sure that he was.

At the police station she demanded to see Colonel García. She demanded to see her husband. She demanded information about her son. She looked fierce, and beautiful, and I thought: perhaps she is not yet lost to us, perhaps she will be the savior of us all. The captain ignored her at first, but then he had an assistant make a telephone call, and in a short time armed police began to come and go, briskly, with purpose, and suddenly my mother was told to come this way.

Colonel García was smoking a cigar, his feet propped up on an open desk drawer. He did not rise and he did not offer her a seat. "What a noisy American woman you are," he said. "You must stop bothering my friend the ambassador. You must stop demanding information on your husband and your son. You are making a great nuisance of yourself." He pushed back in his chair and flicked the ash from his cigar. "This is a republic of law, señora. If you obey the law, you have nothing to fear. Yes, this is so. Your husband is simply a traitor to our state. And we have reason to believe that your son, he too, is a traitor. But they must be investigated. They must, as we say, be detained." He paused a moment and then drew heavily on his cigar. "You must learn a little patience, señora. Patience is a great virtue." He dismissed her. Furious, frightened, she went straight to the American embassy, where, just as she had begun to fear, no one was willing to see her.

That night my mother and I made no pretense of eating. She went to her bedroom with a bottle of brandy; I sat in the living room, listening to music but thinking only of Virgilio.

I thought first of all the distinctions I had been taught by the nuns—love and lust, premarital and postmarital sex, mortal and venial sin, culpability for sin, the malice of sin, sins of commission, of omission, of desire. And then I thought— and realized it was true—that there had been no sin at all between me and Virgilio. We were two people huddling together against the dark and the danger. We were, for one brief second, holding back death.

And I saw then, as if in a vision, that my own death would be long and terrible and triumphant.

Sometime after midnight my mother's door opened and she came into the living room. She blinked against the light for a moment and then she spoke to me, her voice broken, her speech slurred. "Come with me," she said. "We'll leave this place. You and me and Mimi. Jorge is dead; they've killed him; they've tortured him and killed him. And your brother . . ." She broke down and sobbed for a minute. But then she went to the liquor cabinet and poured herself another drink and, as if she had returned to good sense, she began again, "Come with me, María. They've killed your father and your brother and they'll kill us too. There is a curse on this place, there is a curse on us." But finally she saw the coldness in my eyes and the anger in my face, and she stopped. She took her drink to her bedroom and after a while I could hear her packing things in a suitcase. "My jewelry," I heard her say, "and cash, and . . ." I went to my room.

The next morning, incredibly, she was sober and full of

purpose. "I am going to the American embassy," she said, "and then to the police station. If they will not see me and if they will not tell me about Jorge and Miguel, I am coming back here for my suitcase and passport and for you. I will fly to Washington. I want you to come with me. But with you or without you, María, I am going." The housekeeper arrived then and my mother, without another word, put Mimi into her arms and left.

That was this morning. And on this one day, the gods who decide our fates decided mine and Virgilio's and Miguel's.

An hour after my mother left the house, the Guardia arrived. From where I stood in the living room, I saw them push past the housekeeper and, though I wanted to run, I went toward them. "You have no right to be in this house," I said. "Your presence here is strictly illegal."

"Search the place," the lieutenant said, ignoring me. And to the housekeeper, he said, "Save yourself trouble, old woman. Go home." And then he sat on my mother's watered silk sofa and put his feet up on the coffee table. He lit a cigar. "It's your brother we are interested in," he said finally. "Not you."

From the bedrooms I could hear furniture being banged and pushed, drawers torn open and slammed shut, laughter.

Mimi had crawled into my arms and was snuggled against me, whimpering softly. "Make that Yankee dog stop that," the lieutenant said. "It is a very annoying dog. Things that weak and whimpering have no right to live. Don't you agree, señorita? The weak should be stomped out."

The soldiers had finished their search and they had not found Miguel. "Take her in for questioning," the lieutenant said. "I myself will have a look."

The interrogation was like the previous one, only much longer. Where was my brother hiding, and why? Who was Virgilio Bellorin? Why did I go each day to the cathedral?

For whose photograph was I looking? And again, where was my brother hiding, and why? The soldiers took turns questioning me, and near the end Colonel García looked in, smiled, and said, "Your father sends his best wishes." Shortly afterward, I was released and allowed to return home.

I knew what I would find there and I thought I would not be able to bear it. But we can bear anything, if we must.

My mother's room was chaos. Her twin lamps had been broken and drawers had been turned out onto the floor and the entire room was strewn with her clothes, but the bed was neat, the spread smooth, and where the pillow should have been there was her suitcase. Inside the suitcase, of course, was Mimi's body. Her throat had been slit and her fur was matted with blood. I think it was then that I saw how inevitable my own fate was. I closed the suitcase and put it under the bed.

I telephoned the embassy. No, they had no news of my mother. Yes, she did say she was returning to the States. No, they did not know if she had actually left. I telephoned the airport, but they could not release passenger lists. I paced from room to room for nearly an hour and then I telephoned the number Miguel had given to me. "I am desperate to see a Marx Brothers movie," I said. "I am dying to see one, any one; it does not have to be *A Night at the Opera*. Do you understand?" They understood, but nonetheless it was a wrong number. And then, in minutes, a woman called and said, did I know that Hitchcock's *Vertigo* was playing at the Cid; if I hurried, I could make the eight o'clock showing.

I prayed all the way to the theater. The cab was slow and the driver insisted upon talking and I kept saying, "Hurry, hurry, please. If I am late, if I am late . . ." but I could not imagine what would happen if I were late.

I bought my ticket and was standing in the dark at the head of the aisle, letting my eyes adjust, hoping Miguel would appear, when suddenly there was a scuffle in the row to my right: the sound of a punch and then a gasp and feet kicking against the floor. Two Guardia yanked the body of a young man out of the row of seats and into the light of the lobby. His face was bloody, his jacket torn. Miguel, I said to myself, sick with fear. But it was not Miguel; it was Virgilio. I watched as they threw him into the red Toyota van and then, stupid, stunned, I went back inside and waited through *Vertigo,* praying for the dead and dying.

. . .

It is almost over. I walked home through the streets where no one walks. A car would slow and follow me for a block and then turn away. And then another car. And another. Police cars. Guardia cars. Assassination cars. And I walked. At home I let myself into the darkened apartment and sat by the window looking out on the street. It was some time before I realized that the long black car that had been stationed there was at last gone. Why? Because we no longer mattered to them? Who could say.

I must have fallen asleep because all at once Miguel was in the room with me. I cried in his arms, and he let me cry, and after a long time, he said, "It is not over yet. Father, Mother, Virgilio. We will be next." I stopped crying then and I kissed him. I clung to him, pressed myself into him. "Yes, yes," I said. He held me; he held me back. "All right," he said at last, and we made love, my brother and I, as if we could somehow crush ourselves into just one person, become one body, one soul.

Afterward he asked me if I had done this with Virgilio.

"Yes," I said. "I loved him."

"Good," he said, and after a moment, "He was my lover too."

The police, when they came, found us in the kitchen having tea. They put Miguel in one car, me in another, and drove off in different directions. They brought me to this leafy hill and did these things to me. The first one who raped me started to slice off my left breast, but the others wanted to have me while I still had my breasts, so they made him wait until they were all finished. And then they cut the star around my sex. And the cross on my face. They must do these things for courage, to be able to go on. Always they violate sex. Always they put the sign of the cross on their murders. Always they silence the dead mouth.

But mine they will not silence, for I have seen my fate. I will rise from this leafy hill, I will ascend from this body, and I will soar above them like some terrible bird of night.

I will not be a picture in the archbishop's palace, not another faceless one. I will be virgin once again. Cleansed in my own blood, my breasts lucent, and in my throat a triumphant cry, I will sprout wings of bronze and I will course through the night; at dawn I will hover above them, the murdered, the defiled, the dying; I will draw them to me; and I will draw the evil and the sick and the depraved and I will assume them, in my breast, in my loins, in the star they carved on me and in the cross upon my face; I will take them into myself and they will be transformed, made whole, all one.

And at the last it will be well.

FOR THE BEST IN CONTEMPORARY AMERICAN FICTION

☐ WHITE NOISE
Don DeLillo

The New Republic calls *White Noise* "a stunning performance from one of our most intelligent novelists." This masterpiece of the television age is the story of Jack Gladney, a professor of Hitler Studies in Middle America, whose life is suddenly disrupted by a lethal black chemical cloud.

326 pages   ISBN: 0-14-007702-2

☐ IRONWEED
William Kennedy

William Kennedy's Pulitzer Prize-winning novel is the story of Francis Phelan — ex-ball-player, part-time gravedigger, and full-time drunk.

228 pages   ISBN: 0-14-007020-6

☐ LESS THAN ZERO
Bret Easton Ellis

This phenomenal best-seller depicts in compelling detail a generation of rich, spoiled L.A. kids on a desperate search for the ultimate sensation.

208 pages   ISBN: 0-14-008894-6

☐ THE LAST PICTURE SHOW
Larry McMurtry

In a small town in Texas during the early 1950s, two boys act out a poignant drama of adolescence — the restless boredom, the bouts of beer-drinking, and the erotic fantasies.   *220 pages   ISBN: 0-14-005183-X*

FOR THE BEST IN CONTEMPORARY AMERICAN FICTION

☐ **THE WOMEN OF BREWSTER PLACE**
A Novel in Seven Stories
Gloria Naylor

Winner of the American Book Award, this is the story of seven survivors of an urban housing project — a blind alley feeding into a dead end. From a variety of backgrounds, they experience, fight against, and sometimes transcend the fate of black women in America today.
192 pages   ISBN: 0-14-006690-X

☐ **STONES FOR IBARRA**
Harriet Doerr

An American couple comes to the small Mexican village of Ibarra to reopen a copper mine, learning much about life and death from the deeply faithful villagers.   *214 pages   ISBN: 0-14-007562-3*

☐ **WORLD'S END**
T. Coraghessan Boyle

"Boyle has emerged as one of the most inventive and verbally exuberant writers of his generation," writes *The New York Times*. Here he tells the story of Walter Van Brunt, who collides with early American history while searching for his lost father.   *456 pages   ISBN: 0-14-009760-0*

☐ **THE WHISPER OF THE RIVER**
Ferrol Sams

The story of Porter Osborn, Jr., who, in 1938, leaves his rural Georgia home to face the world at Willingham University, *The Whisper of the River* is peppered with memorable characters and resonates with the details of place and time. Ferrol Sams's writing is regional fiction at its best.
528 pages   ISBN: 0-14-008387-1

☐ **ENGLISH CREEK**
Ivan Doig

Drawing on the same heritage he celebrated in *This House of Sky*, Ivan Doig creates a rich and varied tapestry of northern Montana and of our country in the late 1930s.   *338 pages   ISBN: 0-14-008442-8*

☐ **THE YEAR OF SILENCE**
Madison Smartt Bell

A penetrating look at the varied reactions to a young woman's suicide exactly one year later, *The Year of Silence* "captures vividly and poignantly the chancy dance of life." (*The New York Times Book Review*)
208 pages   ISBN: 0-14-011533-1